Blood Clay

BLOOD CLAY

A Novel

VALERIE NIEMAN

PRESS 53
Winston-Salem

Press 53
PO Box 30314
Winston-Salem, NC 27130

First Edition

Cover design and book layout by Kevin Morgan Watson

Cover image Copyright © 2011 by Dorothy O'Connor
www.dorothyoconnor.com

Library of Congress Control Number: 2011900887

Printed on acid-free paper
ISBN 978-1-935708-22-3

To the memory of my grandmothers,
to the loving community of family and friends,
and to Jack

CHAPTER ONE

The dark, her grandmother used to reassure her, was gentle. Tracey Gaines stood under the supermarket's awning and saw the stars, a few strong white points in the blackness beyond the parking lot lights. The air was chilly, but the trees were leafing out and the mulch between the nandina bushes smelled strongly of pine.

She pushed the cart down the ramp and along the row of cars.

A black woman with cropped hair and a bulky nylon wind-suit was standing between Tracey's car and a big Chevy with a peeling vinyl top. Tracey went around to the other side, so as not to hurry her. She opened the passenger door and set the bags of groceries on the seat. The cans rolled and slithered in the plastic, settled against each other.

When she stood up, the woman was still between the cars. She turned her head and looked straight at Tracey.

A jolt of connection made her look away and then look back. The woman's gaze hadn't shifted, her eyes huge, all dark iris, all pupil.

"Hello," Tracey said tentatively. "Can I help you?"

"Car won't start." The woman's voice, low-pitched anyway, was barely audible over the cars on the boulevard.

Tracey closed the passenger door, clattered the empty cart over to the corral, and came back. The other woman slid into her car and turned the key. The engine turned over with a slow growl but didn't catch.

"Sounds like the battery." Tracey bent down to talk with the woman and saw over her shoulder a baby bundled in the car seat and in the back seat, a girl wearing a white coat with blue zippers. She'd seen the little girl standing at the bus stop holding a thin sweater close to her bones, and that very night had pulled the coat off the rack at Wal-Mart.

"Hi, Lakesha."

"Hello, Miss Gaines."

"I saw you playing soccer in class last week. You were really good."

Lakesha smiled and put her face down, shy at the attention.

Tracey turned back to her mother, a woman she didn't know, just a face behind a windshield, a name she had looked up, Orenna Sipe. Mother of Lakesha. The apple roundness of their faces was alike, mother and daughter, but where the child's showed a persistent joy, the mother's was unexpressive.

"Do you want to jump it?" she asked.

"I ain't got no cables."

"I do." Tracey unlocked the trunk, pulled out the Highway Emergency box and lifted the never-used cables from their space between the flares and the tire inflater. If you were prepared, she believed, you'd never need the things, but drive five miles without a spare and a nail will find your tire.

Instructions were printed on a plastic tag. Tracey read them as Orenna felt around under the edge of the hood and popped it. The hinges squealed. The batteries were nested close enough so the cables reached. She opened the brass jaws and clamped them on the battery terminals, following the diagram.

"Wait, now, until I start mine."

Tracey started her car, the smooth rush of the engine and the blurt of someone talking too loudly from the radio. She jabbed the power button, looked over at the other woman. Then she motioned to her, turn the key.

Orenna Sipe's engine ground, coughed, sputtered. Finally it caught.

Tracey got out and unhooked the cables, shut each hood as Orenna kept hitting the gas, the car rocking each time she did, blue smoke coming out of the rear. Tracey smiled at her, happy the car had started, but the other woman's face was closed up, as though she had to work at pumping gas through the engine.

She leaned in at the window. "It should be OK now."

"Thank you." Orenna's head dipped.

"I'm headed home. Do you want me to follow you?"

Orenna said nothing, her face still lowered. Tracey could see only the gleaming corner of her eye. The car roared again. Orenna shifted, each gear ratcheting into place, then a clunk as she hit Drive. Tracey stepped back, the cables still draped over her arm as the car rolled out of the parking space.

Lakesha lifted her hand in the back seat, not waving, just the cupped palm of her hand held up near the window. Her mother hit the gas and roared out of the parking lot trailed by the smell of burned oil.

Truculent. The word came to Tracey as she coiled the jumper cables back into their box. Truculent, the woman was, like her students, anger that just floated out there and landed on whatever was closest.

* * * * *

It was a 20-minute drive from the county seat to her home near Taberville. The road rolled itself out in front of her headlights, between corridors of trees that opened into farmland. A thin moon showed fields of stubble, other fields turned last fall and awaiting the plow and the high-crowned rows where tobacco plants would be set.

She turned off the five-lane onto a winding state route. It had been farmland two hundred years ago; it was pretty much farmland now. Tobacco barns leaned in front of old houses, often with trailers or doublewides set beside, and new metal curing sheds and all the technology of smoke that she had never known before moving South.

Left again at Rutledge Crossroads, where the onetime general store stood back, reticent, the tin roof and metal advertising signs holding together rotting timbers. She crossed a handful of bridges where the river snaked back and forth and streams came down to join it. Landmarks: the Southern States sign, "Jesus wept" painted on the side of a barn, a billboard for fire insurance. She slowed as she came to the Downey Trailer Homes Park No. 1, a row of narrow white trailers, the first five dark. They rented by the month, and soon the migrant workers would be arriving to fill up the court. The sixth trailer, where the Sipes family lived, had a bare yellow bug light burning above the metal stairs but no other sign of life. Now she felt guilty, that she hadn't insisted on following them home.

Why was Orenna so hostile? Tracey had worked that over on the drive, keeping the radio off, thinking. Was she angry about the coat? Was that something to be angry about, such a simple thing, to see a child standing cold and give her something bright and warm?

Tracey braked for her lane, the opening like a rabbit-hole in the thick belt of trees. Maybe she should put a reflector out here. She drove slowly into the pure dark under the oaks, easing the car across the washed-out surface, expecting a cat to dart across the lane, as Enoch did just then, skinny and yellow, breaking her headlight beams like a thrown doll.

The house was whiter in the moonlight than in the day, half hidden by cedars that reached to the second-story porch. She'd fallen in love with it, the way it slouched a bit like farmhouses everywhere, settled comfortably among its trees. She bought it on her second visit. First the job and then the house. Another Yankee fleeing snow and ice. And in her case, the cold leavings of a marriage that once promised so much. She often thought women scorned at least had the heat of their indignation to warm them in their beds; when she and Carl parted, even their friendship had cooled to harmless ash.

The house was set cockeyed to the lane, facing what used to be a working farmyard of barn and chicken coop and granary. Tracey drove the circle around a twisted old crape myrtle and parked in front.

As soon as she turned off the engine, they started to come. Just movement, at first, shadows under the shadows of the trees. Then one long-legged cat, braver than the rest, slipped from under the slumping granary and sat down in the open.

"Hello, Garland," she said.

The others held their ground until she lifted the bags from the seat and the crackle of plastic skittered them back. But Garland, his black-and-white markings askew like a tuxedo put on in a panic, stayed.

She went in through the back door, turned on the lights, put away the juice and yogurt. One of the cats meowed—that sounded like Celia, she thought—then a hissing match erupted. She poked her head into the library, or maybe they had once called it a parlor, but it was her workspace now. The answering machine blinked. When she checked the message, it was only static.

Tracey pulled the bag of cat food from the pantry and went down the side steps onto the flagstones that had once floored a summer kitchen. The roof was long ago lopped off but the tarred angle of the roofline still showed on the clapboards.

The cats, six of them tonight, were clustered at a safe distance, farm cats that came attached to the property. She poured nibbles into two beat-up aluminum cake pans, then retreated to the steps and sat down with her hands clasped around her knees. The cats moved in, a motley bunch of calicos, tabbies.

Enoch (blinking as though he were sick) walked with a rolling, bowlegged gait from the extra toes on his front feet. He pawed at his face and she worried about distemper, but when he came closer she saw a line of blood from nose to ear. So he was half the catfight.

"Hey, Celia," she said softly. "Better come get some."

Celia was a calico, a runt that had managed to survive though she still hung back at the food dishes. Right now she was prowling the edges of the pack, as though looking for a way in, though she could have come around to the empty space on the side nearest Tracey. None of them did.

She was taming them, the way Carl taught her to tame chickadees, standing in the Pennsylvania winter with her arm outstretched and her hand filled with seeds. At first the birds would only watch and call, then fly down with a whir of wings and snatch a seed. Finally, trusting, they would grasp a finger with the smallest needle-pricks of claws through woolen mittens and sit on her hand, feeding.

Such a long time. Patience is a virtue, she would repeat as driven snow stung her cheeks and her feet got cold.

Like tonight, she thought wryly, her rear end frozen from sitting on the concrete step, her chest aching from breath held.

Tracey stood and took a step toward the cats crunching at the bowls. Ears flicked and the most skittish fled. Another step and the cats bounded away, disappearing under the car and the bushes, all but Garland, who trotted out of reach and sat down, looking at her.

"Just want to be left alone, huh?"

She went inside and turned off the outside light. As her eyes adjusted, she saw them run back, hungry, confident with the return of darkness.

CHAPTER TWO

Esse quam videri. Dave Fordham glanced up at the motto carved in marble above the portico: To be, rather than to seem. Fine sentiment, here in red-dirt Saul County. Tobacco had built this school, a fake Gothic cathedral shaded by its willow oaks in the middle of the flat, hot fields. Under the portico, a heavy pair of arched doors, blackened oak, more Old World baloney and more Latin: In the half-moon space above the doors, carved letters and tobacco leaves entwined, faded gold leaf on the school motto: *Magna est veritas et prevalebit.* Truth is strong and will prevail.

They didn't teach Latin here any longer.

The door, heavy as it was, opened easily, the noise shouldering against him from inside. The vaulted main hallway echoed like a cave. Kids slammed lockers and yelled, the morning noise of any bunch of adolescents thickened to a toxic stew by anger and frustration.

"Hey!"

A tennis ball sailed past his ear.

Dave didn't turn to see who had thrown it. The faces would all be blank, the eyes flat. Even the babies on their mothers' hips seemed to know what was expected at A.O. Miller Alternative School.

Everyone funneled through the front entrance with its metal detectors and security camera. The children of field hands, here to learn English. Pregnant girls and new mothers headed for the nursery in the annex. The behaviorally impaired and the emotionally damaged. Students with learning disabilities who should be elsewhere but who had pulled a knife on a classmate or been busted for selling drugs behind the Texaco. The school board, like any authority faced with insoluble problems, had decided those problems were best handled by placing them in one basket. With the lid firmly on.

Outside the principal's office, a student Dave taught last year sat aslant the vinyl bench, his head leaned against the wall. Dave paused but Trey said nothing, his eyes turned to asphalt.

He went on into the office. "Hey," he said to Ruth. The secretary, new this year, sat with her head cocked back, looking at the computer screen, her gaze uneasily focused through trifocals.

"Hello," she said, without looking at him.

Dave got mail from his cubbyhole: state teachers' newsletter, a brochure on a program in Raleigh, a memo on a fire drill Thursday afternoon. With any luck it would rain.

When he went out, the school cop was standing over Trey, who had changed neither his slump nor that hot slag stare.

Dave walked up the creaking back stairs to the second floor, his damaged right foot heavy on the steps. At his classroom door—"Faggot Fordham" dug into the dark wood where a nameplate should be—he got out his keys and sorted through them one-handed.

He heard her coming before she turned the corner. Tracey Gaines had a certain walk, a kind of slowed quickness he'd tried to characterize: someone who was anxious, trying to walk fast without appearing to do so, or someone eager who equally wanted to hide that fact. She was wearing her usual pants and blazer—Dave didn't think he'd ever seen her wear a skirt. Her long hair looked red today, vibrant, swinging across the shoulders of the green jacket.

"Hi, Dave."

"Hey." She already had her key out, bracing an overstuffed portfolio under her arm, and he started to say something and move toward her but she was gone, slow-fast, like slow motion of a pitcher uncoiling a fastball, or a hummingbird's beat turned into heavy oaring.

He got his door open and went in. Nothing to hurry for. He turned on the lights, though the sun beat through the tall windows. The janitors had neatly lined the desks up after sweeping but disarray lingered in the bookcase and the resource file and would creep back into the room during the day. Dave snapped open his briefcase and laid out his grade book, lesson planner, two pens. He sat down, square behind the heavy wooden desk, then tilted the chair slowly onto its back legs and looked up at the exposed pipes and the bird nest in the joint between pipe and hanger. The window had been cracked open all summer long, forgotten he supposed, so that the chattering wrens came in and out, made their home, only to be evicted with brooms and shouting when classes started.

His students wandered in. Rikk, Jonah, Jim, Deon. Dewayne, who threw himself into the too-small desk with a screech of metal chair feet across the floor. He pushed his thick legs far into the aisle.

The bell rang. Dave waited. Edgar strolled in. He checked them off, six of the nine in class today, better than average. Then he handed out worksheets.

It was better having all boys, easier to choose materials. This one was about motorcycles. Two pages of text to read, a simple story about a kid helping his father fix his Harley, and then a page of questions. What was wrong with the motorcycle? Why was the father happy?

Edgar left his sheet where it fell on his desk, sat with his face averted, staring out the window at the parking lot and the road.

Jim Pennell looked down at his hands in his lap. A swipe of hair fell across his eyes. His plaid shirt flopped at the wrists.

"You'll like this," Dave urged. "Your dad has a motorcycle, doesn't he?"

Jim nodded.

He tried to encourage the boy, who seemed not quite hopeless enough for this place. If he did his work and avoided fights, he might make it back to his regular school, to a regular classroom and maybe someday a diploma.

The Pennell kid leaned over his paper, right arm encircling it, left hand struggling with the pen as he wrote his name at the top. Eventually all the students except Edgar scratched away, completing the worksheets.

Dave led them through a discussion, question by question, cajoling, challenging, playing the fool a bit because a sarcastic grin was at least a response. It was a step away from stand-up, a one-man show, and just as grueling.

"What does the writer tell us?" he asked. "What do we know about the father?" He leaned toward the class with his head bent forward. "Rikk, why don't you start us off?"

The boy looked down at his paper. Dave waited. "I guess," Rikk drawled, "he ain't been working."

Dave turned to the blackboard, too quickly; his nerveless foot caught the garbage can and sent it spinning away. A couple of the kids laughed snarkily, but most just shifted position, silent as he wrote "out of work." Their silence unnerved him. Like Dewayne. Dewayne never said anything, never did anything, but he knew when he turned around that the tackle-sized freshman would be glaring at him.

By early lunch he was exhausted. His back ached. He waited until the boys were on their way and then stretched, balancing on his good foot, grunting as the muscles spasmed and then eased.

He followed them down the back stairs to the cafeteria, in the basement like the kitchen of a manor house. The cooks labored in steam and the students shoveled the food in under flickering lights. And always, the teachers standing monitor—he raised his hand to Earl Reynolds at the next set of double doors.

Tracey was monitoring the girls' probation table, three sullen teens who were not allowed to speak or listen to music during their lunch period. He caught her eye and pointed up the hall. One of the girls, her hair spiked into red points, caught the exchange and laughed out loud, showing all her teeth. She made a kissing mouth and the other girls shrieked.

Jesus. One sign of adult weakness and they're all over it.

He avoided looking at Tracey for the rest of the lunch period, and when the bell rang he lingered and made conversation with Earl about his fruit trees. When he caught up with Tracey in the lounge, she had started a new pot of coffee and had her lunch bag open.

"I don't know about punishment for *them*," she said, plunking an apple on the coffee table, "but it's damn sure punishment for *me*."

He nodded.

"They twitch, and they peel the polish off their nails, and they scrape their knives on the plates."

Dave leaned back into the flattened cushions on the couch.

Teachers drifted in and out, a word here or there, the refrigerator door clunking shut as they took out sodas and microwave meals. The usual trio, George, "Tick," and Angelo, pulled up at the round table and began to argue NASCAR.

Dave and Tracey ate in mutual silence. It was a blessing. They set their coffee cups on a yellowed copy of *Education Week*.

He watched how she ate, short attacks on the hard green apple, her teeth showing white as she took each bite and her wide forehead wrinkling as though she pondered the wisdom of that bite. Everything about her was watchful. He thought of an animal brought into a new environment, and how that wariness was a survival skill. She'd joined the faculty last fall but at first kept to herself, scarcely a word out of her. She never loosened up until after Christmas break. One day in the lounge, she had just started asking him about local history, the families, how names had come to roads and towns.

Finished, she folded her bag and stuffed it down inside her purse.

"Did I tell you about the barefoot boy?" She touched the corner of her mouth, removing a crumb.

He shook his head.

"Last Friday, this kid comes to class barefoot. Now, he has shoes. God knows what this was all about. Before he could even get to his seat, this other kid—Andy Bowers, you know him—came over in those big yellow brogans and stomped on his foot."

Dave was thinking how she said brogans, stress on the first syllable, strange. Here you said BRO-GANS, evenly as two feet hitting the ground.

"And they threw some punches. Andy ended up with a bloody nose, and the SRO came and hauled them both out in handcuffs." She leaned over, tapped him on the arm to get all his attention, "Handcuffs. Like criminals."

"Yeah." Dave looked at her fingers on his arm. No rings. Not even a watch. She took her hand away and sat back.

"Any other school would have done in-school suspension," she said. "Zero tolerance."

That was the phrase these days. This was the place you ended up with when you multiplied by zero. Dave was disquieted by the atmosphere, by the school resource officer always rocking on his heels in the hall. He could have told the administrators it didn't work, that metal detectors and harsher punishments were an illusion of security. That this school would become not the place to which problems were exiled, but from which they spread. Like that red-brick institution where he'd first taught, where cops walked beats in the halls and sullen students grew more sullen, while the good ones stayed away. Students had sex behind the curtains of the disused auditorium. The bad guys passed pistols through the fence, broke in to hide drugs in the locker room ceilings, lay in wait.

" … screwed up."

He was startled back to the conversation, realizing he'd lost track of what Tracey was talking about. He made a noncommittal hum.

"It's just lack of maintenance," she said. "Paint, mostly. Caulking. The well was silted in, never was a septic system. But the house itself is in good shape."

"Sounds like a lot of work." That place on Burnt Cabin Road would be a handful for a family of carpenters. He wondered why she had bought it.

"Keeps me busy," she said, eerily like an answer. "There's not a lot else for a girl to do down here in the Land o' Cotton."

"Tobacco."

"Whatever. No offense—I know you're from around here."

"You don't see a Confederate flag on my car, do you?"

She gave him that direct hard stare that he'd seen from people in the North, the rural small-town North, not the city, where you avoided other people's eyes. Her eyes were clear blue; she could give a real Yankee stare, the look of someone who was well aware she might be cheated.

Tracey wasn't like the women he had grown up with. She wore her independence right out in the open; she didn't slow up or defer. It was nice to talk with her in the course of the day, but he didn't delude himself about their friendship.

The bell rang and the noise in the hall swelled, classes changing accompanied by yelling, primal outcries, an erratic anarchic sound, these country-bred kids already with a street-corner feel to their bones, mass market anonymity erasing their jug ears and niblet teeth.

Tracey tucked her portfolio under her arm and he picked up his satchel.

"Onward, Christian soldiers," he said.

She grinned, opened the door, and they pushed into the stream of kids and adults, skinny boys and men with beards, girls chunky with pre-pubescent fat, girls chunky with post-pubescent pregnancies. All students. Pupils. A term more appropriate than it might seem, as it originally meant orphans. Children adrift.

They went up the back stairs, giving way for the one kid always pushing against the flow, and as they reached the second landing, a boy yelled out, "Hey, Old Baldy's got a girlfriend."

Tracey glanced at him. Dave felt the flush moving up his neck and started babbling. "Yeah, the latest. Seems like a new name every week. Someone wrote on the blackboard that Fordham doesn't have a hair …."

And he stopped, realizing he'd dug himself a hole. *Not a hair on his ass.* He wondered if she traced where the sentence was headed.

Tracey walked to the door of her room, and as he started to trudge past, she reached over and squeezed his arm.

That afternoon, Dave struggled to teach alliteration.

"Not rhyme," he emphasized. "Not the sound at the end of the word, the sound at the beginning."

Not ass and grass, the first spring greenery so clear under the sun. Not ball and call, the children from the new K-4 across the road shrieking as they tumbled after a soccer ball on the beaten field.

Inside, his students leaned back in their chairs, dulled by the dull beige tiles and dull mustardy walls.

"Land," he said. "Leaves, less, loam, loan, leaving."

On wide-spreading land like this you should be able to grow anything, but couldn't grow these kids. If you cut them loose in the fields, they would all die, sit down and die in the midst of plenty they couldn't see any more than they could understand the last sound that came out of their mouths.

CHAPTER THREE

Tracey was chilled when she got in her car, having seen the last of the students onto the buses and the last of the buses onto Highway 343.

The bright day had faded. Despite the sun in the tops of the trees, the wind had kicked up and purple clouds were spreading from the north like a new-risen ridge of mountains. The NPR announcer spoke low and clear, no crisis so great it couldn't be reported in calmness. National Therapy Radio, she called it, the same kind of soothing voice, same impersonal reassurance. She tried to think what she had at home for dinner, but couldn't focus. Something. With a bundle of papers to grade and a test to prepare, food would be secondary. There was something leftover and still in the pot, chili, spaghetti, she couldn't remember.

Tracey recognized her old enemy, the exhaustion that made her sit down on the couch, then lie down, then nap and wake more tired than before. It chewed up her concentration and swallowed her confidence. She couldn't place the reason for it. Winter was gone, and though this evening the clouds had quickly gathered up the sun, the days were starting to get longer. No particular memory was attached to this time of year, no happy time with Carl nor sadness of some loss, nothing to pull her down.

She turned onto the secondary road, pinewoods on the left, fields and a farm on the right. The parking lights weren't enough and she flipped on the headlights.

She caught up with the bus on Burnt Cabin Road, at the usual place. No. 41 had taken its circuitous route through the county and was nearly empty as it wallowed over the low hills. Tracey backed off the accelerator, no good place to pass now as the road curved and looped.

Two kids got off at a shotgun house painted an amazing shade of gloss marine blue.

Four children scattered to waiting cars at Macklin Crossroads.

The next stop was the trailer court, for Lakesha, and then the bus would roll past her driveway empty.

The Stop! sign swung out and the bus lights flashed. Tracey listened to an interview with a man who played the glass armonica. She stared out her side window. Three, no, four big dogs loped across a field, headed somewhere. Not hounds—a massive dark dog was in the lead, head up as though following something by sight rather than scent.

Lakesha hopped off the last step and went back up the road to the row of mailboxes. The driver kept his lights flashing while she pulled down the door, peered inside, then pushed the rusty door closed with both hands. She trudged back to the trailer park lane. Her white jacket glowed in the dim light. Tracey was disappointed to see it swinging open, unzipped.

In her rearview mirror, Tracey saw the dogs again, breaking into a run as they crossed the road behind her car. She looked over, expecting to see deer in the plowed field on the other side, but it was empty.

The school bus lurched forward, over the rise. She let off the brake, wanting to be home.

Movement caught her eye again; the dogs were running hard.

Lakesha dawdled up the sandy road, swinging her book bag by its strap.

Tracey put down the window: "Lakesha!"

The girl waved, then opened up a smile and started back toward the highway. Tracey kept an eye on the dogs, worried they would frighten her.

"Hey, dogs!" Tracey yelled. She whistled, but the dogs didn't heed.

Now Lakesha saw them. She shrieked and flailed her arms. The dogs angled toward the girl, and now she began to run.

She threw her bag at them and the lead dog snatched it up, shook it hard one time the way dogs kill groundhogs, one hard snap, then tossed it aside.

The car had drifted almost into the ditch. Tracey turned the wheel and hit the gas, honked the horn, screamed out the window as Lakesha stumbled backward, fell, and the dogs were on her.

Tracey inched the car forward, trying to back the dogs off, but when one moved the others came on and she couldn't tell how close she was to where Lakesha had gone down. As Tracey opened the door a dog pushed its lug head into the gap, snapping, snarling, with blood on its muzzle. She slammed the door hard on its skull twice before it howled and retreated.

Her knees were shaking. Her hands were numb.

She honked and honked. The bus was gone. The trailers were dark, even the one at the end where Lakesha lived, the Chevy in the drive but the house closed up, the drapes pulled.

A black dog clawed the door, a machine-gun sound, and lunged into the open window, teeth bared. Tracey threw herself across the seat, out of reach.

No one on the road.

No one in the raw red fields.

The dogs somewhere, out of sight, and she heard a growl but nothing from the girl.

Tracey hit reverse, bouncing back onto the road and then shifting, accelerating as she turned into her lane, the car banging over the ruts, her head hitting the roof. She stopped nearly against the porch, digging in her pocketbook for the keys as she ran up the steps. She banged open the screen door, jammed, jabbed, twisted the key in. 911.

"Saul County Communications," the dispatcher drawled. "Is this an emergency?"

"Yes. Yes! Dogs attacking a little girl. Downey Trailer Park. Burnt Cabin Road. Downey Park."

"Are you with the child?"

"Yes. No. I'm calling. I'm a neighbor."

She heard the dispatcher summon police, ambulance, the repeated address, all calm, steady, as she dropped the phone.

Tracey slewed the car around the drive and headed back to the trailer park. All she could see was the white coat, Lakesha's face, the snarling dogs.

At the lane into the silent trailer park, nothing.

The dogs were gone. The girl, gone.

She sat for a moment. Had she imagined it? She opened the door. Cold night was closing in; wind bent over the bleached heads of last year's weeds.

No dogs. No Lakesha. The trailers dark.

Tracey got out, leaving the car running, the headlights fanning across the road and the first of the trailers. She heard the repeated chime from the open door, heard sand grind under her heels, heard an airplane droning toward the county airstrip. She saw where her wheels had spun as she backed out. Then a dark streak—she bent, touched it, black on the coarse sand but when she raised her hand to the headlight beam, her fingertips were red.

Farther along, the sand was trampled and torn, mixed with blood, all the way to the ditch bank. She looked and saw Lakesha, half in the water.

Tracey slid down the bank. The wind's moan was cut off here, and she could hear Lakesha breathing, a raspy, bubbly sound. When she touched the girl, Lakesha moved away, and she could see that the dogs had torn her throat and hands. Fresh blood washed out of the wounds.

She was afraid to lift her legs out of the ditch water, afraid to do anything. She took off her blazer and draped it over Lakesha. Then she heard the siren, the ambulance coming from the Taberville substation. Tracey sat on the cold bank and kept her hand on her arm until the ambulance driver, boots sliding into the water, pulled her out of the way and let the paramedic reach Lakesha.

"Are you OK?" he asked, his voice like his hands, only half gentle.

She nodded her head, yes, and stood where the man put her.

The paramedic had tossed her blazer aside and was working with a flashlight clamped between her knees. The woman's rear end stuck up ludicrously but her movements were efficient as she checked Lakesha for broken bones, pressed compression bandages into place, inserted an IV.

"What's her name?" she called.

"Lakesha. Sipe."

"Does she live here?"

Tracey pointed to the end of the road, but they weren't looking at her. "She lives in the last trailer."

The driver came back with a gurney. The wheels rattled on the gravel like dice in a box, like bones.

Another siren, blue lights flashing in the dusk, and from the radio in the ambulance she heard the deputy checking in. He pulled up, cut the siren but left the lights going.

Tracey raised her head at a squawk of metal on metal from down the road. Lakesha's mother stood on the landing of her trailer, peering, her hand shielding her face from the bare bulb overhead.

"Oh Jesus," she cried as she came down the steps. "Oh Jesus," the words pacing her as she started to run, "Oh Jesus," and then as she got closer and spotted the stretcher coming up out of the ditch, the words rose into a wordless shriek that ran a chill down Tracey's back.

The deputy intercepted her. Orenna Sipe beat on his shoulders with her fists and pushed him a step backward, forcing her way toward her daughter.

"Lakesha," she cried, and the girl's head turned just a bit.

The paramedic looked back, her face twisted and pale.

"Mrs. Sipe," the deputy said, calm.

"Lakesha!"

The ambulance crew raised the stretcher up and slid it into the bay, the IV drip held high, the paramedic climbing in beside the girl.

"I was asleep," Orenna cried. "I laid down with my baby."

"Mrs. Sipe, if you'd …"

"Asleep, oh Jesus." She looked over the deputy's shoulder at Tracey, a flat look as though she didn't know who she was, as though she couldn't imagine why she was here. And then the paramedic said something to the deputy, and he helped Orenna climb in beside her daughter, where she sat rocking and rocking as the doors closed and he slammed his palm twice against the metal to send them off.

Now the deputy turned his attention to her.

"You're the one who called. The neighbor."

She nodded. "Tracey Gaines."

"Sergeant Findley." He wasn't one of the deputies she had seen come to the school to take disruptive students away.

She rubbed her arms, feeling the cold now through her thin blouse, and what seemed like a few drops of rain. She stared at the book bag where the dog had thrown it.

"Let's do the report where it's warm," he said.

They got in the cruiser and he started it up, ran the heater. There was a den-like smell of a car someone lived in. Tracey watched rain spatter on the windshield as he sorted through forms on a clipboard and moved one to the top. He went through name, address, how long she'd lived there. "How do you know the victim?"

"I teach at the alternative school and Lakesha's class comes over from the elementary for a session or two. And during the summer she and her mother walked past my house a couple of times."

"And the mother?"

"She works at a sock mill and somewhere else. Lakesha's alone a good bit," she said, then paused, wondering if she was indicting the mother.

"Father?"

"I don't know. I haven't seen anyone."

Then he asked her to tell "in her own words" what had happened. When she first saw the dogs. How she tried to warn Lakesha. How she tried … Tracey felt the word accuse her with each repetition. Tried, tried. The sergeant said nothing as he wrote out the statement in block printing, like a draftsman.

"Can you describe the dogs?"

A Rottweiler, black with rust-colored markings. A brown, brindled one, like a boxer crossed with something else. Those dogs she knew. Then there was a shorter dog, gray, heavy-muscled, with a big head, what she would call a pit bull. And a furry dog like a shepherd or collie. Those she didn't know.

"And whose dogs are those?"

"The two, the big black one and the brindled one, they're …" and she paused before she could say the name, "Artis Pennell's."

He glanced up. "You're sure of that?"

"Yes."

She knew those dogs. For close to a year she'd seen them, riding past in the back of his red Ford pickup, their mouths always open, tongues hanging out. Artis Pennell lived on the family farm that backed up to her land, and they waved as they occasionally passed each other on the road. Neighbors, she thought, with a warm sense of reassurance. Sometimes they'd run into each other in Taberville, or at the county seat, once even in Raleigh in front of a strip mall bagel shop. Then, late last October, it all had changed.

The deputy nudged her with the clipboard. She scrawled her name where he had marked an X.

"You're sure about those dogs, now?"

"Yes. For God's sake, they tried to get me!" He glanced up, his brow wrinkling at the Lord's name used in vain. "They came at me through the car door, into the window! I slammed the door on the brindled one."

He wrote a bit more and signed at the bottom, handed her the pen. Her signature was shaky and small next to his.

"Let's take a look," he said. He pulled out a heavy black flashlight, more a weapon than an implement. The spate of rain had fallen off to a cold drizzle. They crunched back along the road, cut up with boot prints, the wavering wheel tracks of the gurney, the dug-in places where vehicles had made hard turns. The door was still open on her faithful gray Civic, but someone had turned off the engine and laid the keys on the seat. Sergeant Findley shone his light on the seat, wet along the edge, then on the floor, the door frame.

"Those stains on the seat?"

She bit her lip, knowing they came from fast food eaten on the road. "They're old."

There was something red and wet on the rocker panel. The deputy touched it. Not blood, just clay, common Carolina red dirt wet from the rain.

"They stand up on this side?" He half-shut the door and played the beam along it. "You got some scratches here," he said, but his voice showed doubt. Tracey bent closer. She could tell the new marks, some parallel scratches down from the window, but any of the scratches could have been made as easily by grocery carts or branches along the road.

"You'd better get in." She slid into the seat. The officer looked inside again, maybe for a clump of dog hair, maybe something else.

"You OK to get home?"

"Yes. Thank you."

He shut the door after her, and motioned for her to fasten her seat belt. She followed the police car out.

In front of her house, she sat in the car for a long time, her head against the steering wheel and her hands gripped to stop their shaking. Over and over, Lakesha fell and the black dog leaped. And the brindled dog jammed its head into the open car door, blood on its muzzle.

They were Artis's dogs, yes, she was sure, she remembered them slobbering over the side of the truck last October as she went into the post office. The population around Taberville was too small and spread-out to allow for route delivery, so people had to pick up their mail. She was waiting on the clerks to finish sorting it into the boxes when Artis Pennell came in, flashing that wide smile.

"Too hot for this late in the year," she offered.

"Yeah, but tobacco's all gone to market and there's only fall plowing." He opened one of the large boxes on the bottom row, lifted a thick stack of mail onto the counter and began to pitch the junk into the trash can with a smooth flick of the wrist.

Tracey had thought about him more and more in recent months. He was a few years older, with a little more gray in his dark hair than in hers, a little bit of paunch. Like her, he was divorced, but with a son. Artis had moved back to his parents' place. They were alike in that, too, turning to country life and what it could do to ease the loss.

The clerk thrust two bills and a Penny-Pincher into her box. Artis was still sorting as she walked past, and she lingered outside, reading a rummage sale notice tacked to the power pole. She smiled when he came out and felt a little jolt when he lingered to talk, his two big dogs behind him panting and turning around in the truck bed.

"How are things coming on the old place?" he asked. His blue eyes were bright, agreeable, nested in crows-feet crinkled against the sun.

"All right. I'm fighting the plumbing right now."

Artis nodded, his lips pursed for a moment as though he were considering something. She plunged ahead, encouraged by the casual way he eased his back away from the side of the truck, refusing to listen to that voice in her head reminding her, no more men, no more men.

"You come over for a glass of sweet tea sometime and I'll show you my handiwork."

His smile faded to an open-mouthed gape. "Oh, honey," he said. "Let's just stay neighbors. You got too much cat in you for a hound like me."

He hadn't laughed, had just pulled himself right away and gotten in his truck, leaving her standing there with her mail sliding out of her hand.

Now Tracey lifted her head from the steering wheel, opened her eyes and stared at the old house until all she could see was a blur of white, but it did no good. She saw the dogs leaping, the dogs leaping. The way Lakesha flinched when she touched her. Finally, she got out of the car and gathered up her books and portfolio.

She was momentarily startled by the movement of the cats under the trees.

She carried the bag of food out and filled their pans, but they seemed more shy than usual and stayed out of range, their eyes green fire and bodies offering no friendship. She went inside, slammed the heavy door, turned the lock, and faced the dark stairs and the cold bedroom and a sleepless night.

Chapter Four

The roadside altar was well under way by the time she left home for school the next morning.

Someone had come in the night and planted a cross made out of white PVC pipe where the attack had happened. It tilted on the side of the road. Tracey looked away, but was drawn back.

She stopped the car. A small teddy bear leaned against the cross, and there were flowers, some stiff plastic, others real, so newly laid that they showed no sign of withering. Somewhere down in the ditch was her green blazer.

Tracey turned on the radio and kept it loud while she drove, for distant but familiar voices, "Morning Edition," the list of day sponsors celebrating children's birthdays and twentieth anniversaries. As she approached the school, she saw yellow ribbons draped from the branches of the skinny Bradford pears in front of the elementary school. A huge yellow rosette was centered on each side of the entrance.

The smooth pavement in the circle by the new building deteriorated as she turned into the parking lots beside the alternative school. She hit broken asphalt—damn—it hadn't been that bad before.

She was early. She had lain in the rumpled bed as the pre-dawn dark thickened. It seemed like it would never break. She tried to identify the birds mimicked in a mockingbird's repeated phrases and tried to forget the repeated phone calls to the hospital last night.

The child was in surgery, the nurse had said, and the family had requested that no information be given out. Later, just a curt, "No information." Tracey had known Lakesha was dead, had known in the chill voice of the nurse, even before the white cross and the yellow ribbons.

Students were subdued, gathered in knots by the lockers, their heads together.

"Ms. Gaines." She turned from her mail cubby to see Principal Harvey Arbogast holding open the door of his office. The Inner Sanctum, the teachers called it, where no one was invited. "Would you join us, please?"

As she came around the counter she saw Dave sitting in the other armchair in front of the desk. He pushed himself halfway to his feet as she came in, head ducked so that she stared into the place where his light brown hair was thinning to scalp, then he sat back with his striped tie askew.

"I wanted to be sure to see you before classes, Ms. Gaines," Arbogast said. He was a black man, punctilious, remote, with manners and a style of dress older than his sixty-odd years. "We were concerned about you this morning. You have heard, I am certain, that Lakesha Sipe has died of her wounds."

Tracey sat down in the other chair, one knee hitting the corner of the big desk and the pain a momentary refuge from the word, *wounds*, from the sound of Dave clearing his throat, from the oppressive walnut-paneled walls and books and volumes and certificates and the solid weight of Arbogast's world. From the news. No, she might assure him, she hadn't heard. In so many words.

"I'm certain you did all you could," he said.

"Yes," Dave said.

Tracey kept rubbing her knee. "I wish I'd had a cell phone," she said.

The principal nodded. "We're all very sorry. I'm certain this is traumatic."

Tracey had feared sleep. She called an old friend in Columbus, someone to talk to, but that tie was long ago frayed and it was hard to get past questions about her ex, about her love life, updates on people she didn't care about any longer. And then she went upstairs and lay down, tried to sleep, tried for hours, wrestling the horror down only to have it spring up and take control of her thoughts. She called the hospital. She watched the light reveal her room, item by item, until at last she had gotten up and made coffee.

"A counselor is over at the elementary school to meet with Lakesha's classmates," the principal said. "There will be an assembly for the school. She also will meet with any of our students individually, if there is a need."

Tracey wondered why Dave was there. He kept looking at her as though he expected her to scream suddenly.

"Ms. Gaines," the principal said. "Have you seen the television this morning?"

"No. I don't own one." He didn't look surprised.

"The owner of the dogs was on the news this morning," Dave said. "Pennell. He was saying those were his kid's dogs and they weren't vicious. That it wasn't his dogs that did it."

"But I know those dogs," she protested.

"We have no doubt that you correctly filed the report," Arbogast said. "But anger, yes, can make a man say wild things." He looked at her over his reading glasses with the sorrow of a man who once said something in anger.

Tracey felt her face go numb. She stared at the commendations ranked on the back wall of Arbogast's office. It wasn't like she was expecting an award, or anything, but she never expected to be doubted at her word. Anxiety rolled over her, insecurity like a cold wave that crushed her against a lightless bottom. Were those his dogs? Was she sure? Was she sure what she saw? When she closed her eyes and remembered the ravening jaws of the brindled dog, she was certain. She wanted to cry with Orenna, oh Jesus, sweet Jesus.

"I had Mr. Fordham join us because I believe you've come to know each other through your room assignments. I thought you might want someone to talk with," Arbogast said, his voice very soft now.

She understood what he didn't say, that in her second semester she was still a stranger in the school and in the town, that Dave was the only person he could identify as her friend.

"Ms. Gaines." She looked up and met the principal's eyes, reddened with that old sorrow or with empathy. "Would you like someone to carry you home?"

Tracey tried to parse the sentence. Carry me. *Coming for to carry me home.* She heard a piano half out of tune, ivory veneer snapped off the center keys, and her aunt singing "Negro spirituals." Carry me home. That's what they said down here. "No, no really. I'm fine. I'd rather be working."

"Very well."

They left Arbogast sitting at his desk, erect as a wax statue on its steel bones, centered behind his spotless desk blotter. The bell had rung and the hallways were mostly empty, although one boy ducked into the restroom when he saw Dave and Tracey come around the corner.

Dave's bad foot clumped hard on the stairs, though he tried to disguise his handicap. "I imagine he'll be back on the noon news," he said. "If you want, we can watch in the AV lab," he said.

She nodded.

"If you need anything, I'm right next door." He paused, his mouth half open as if to say something else.

"Thanks." Tracey didn't know if she wanted to stand here, awkward, or enter that classroom. "You're a good friend."

Dave looked at the floor and she realized that was how he reacted to bad news, looking down and away so as not to face it. He's been kind, she thought, and I must seem awfully cold.

"Dave," she tried again, and he turned back from his waiting classroom, "that means a lot."

He smiled then, an open-hearted, all the lights on, welcome-to-Mayberry smile that lifted her heart despite everything. He doesn't smile nearly enough, Tracey thought.

Her class went stone silent when she walked in. The normal round of giggles, lazily delayed remarks, the usual shuffle of feet on the floor—nothing.

"Good morning."

"Good morning," returned a scattering of voices.

"Yesterday I asked you to think about what women did at this time," she said, as she focused on removing books from her portfolio, setting them out on the desk. "What kind of work did they do around 1870? How is that work different from today?"

Half the class stared at her, their eyes bright and hard as sparrows' eyes. The other half stared at their desks, or out the window.

"How was their work different—Madonna?"

The big girl in the last row turned her face forward, but said nothing.

"Jorge?"

He spread his hands, widened his eyes in a gesture that meant, no habla. The snickers started.

Tracey wasn't going to bring up the subject that roamed the space between her desk and theirs. She pulled out worksheets she'd planned for half the class period, knowing they could dawdle over them for the entire time. Let them. The papers passed from hand to hand along the rows. "And for extra credit, you may write a paragraph to answer the discussion question for today," she added.

She took a new textbook from the bottom drawer, propped it up and read page after page without comprehending a thing. She stared at a map of the Louisiana Purchase until it became totally unfamiliar, the outlines of a newly discovered island.

What a fool I've been.

She had come to know Artis Pennell's son before she met the man. Jim was in her American History I class last fall. He wasn't a bad kid, didn't act up, but never had a word to say in discussions. His homework was completed, but never a bit of extra effort, the reports counted to the exact word (just, very, like, and handfuls of adjectives sprinkled throughout to eke out the length).

When she first ran into the Pennells at the home center, she was balancing a rug atop a load of paint and Jim saw her and came to help steady the load. Artis followed along, pushing a hand truck full of lumber, and his son introduced her, "My teacher, Miss Gaines."

"Looks like we got us some projects," Artis said, nodding toward her cart.

"I may have bitten off more than I can chew," she said. "I appreciate Jim giving me a hand."

"He's not any trouble in class, is he?"

"Not a bit." And that was true. Jim shot her a wary glance, as if waiting for some additional comment, and when none came, he told his father he was going to the truck.

She let Artis go first through the checkout, insisting that since his son was waiting, he should move ahead in the long line snaking toward a single clerk.

"You bought the old Floyd place," he observed. "We live around the back side of the hill, off Eccelston Road. The tobacco farm."

Tracey nodded, though she couldn't place which farm. Tobacco was planted in fields and strips all over the place, and whose it was she couldn't tell.

He looked at her. "I imagine you've met my mother. She's around the back of the property a lot, picking berries and persimmons and such."

"Yes, I've seen her," she said, recalling an old woman in a dress— she had seen her twice, and the woman had waved and called out, and she had lifted her hand in return. They had never talked. "Most of the time I'm working on the house, fixing it up. It needs painting."

"Yeah, I'll bet." He moved his load forward with a casual shove. One two-by-four slid down to land on the wide boards. "Well, the boy and me are back on the home place. Seemed like the thing to do. I didn't think it was good for Jim to grow up in Charlotte without a mother."

She looked closer, thought she read the suffering in his square, sunburned face. His wife must have left him abruptly, one of those hard breaks. She and Carl had settled everything reasonably, equitably, as good friends might. Lover, best friend, companion in her work—all gone at once, a sheaf of papers shuffled together until they were one neat document, signed and notarized.

"I'm just a farmer at heart anyway," he said, and grinned. "Didn't take much for me to get home and put my toes in the dirt. And Mom can use help with the tobacco, even if it is going out fast with the lawsuits and all."

They nudged forward. An old man in front of them had an electrical socket and some wire.

"So where you come from, Miss Gaines?"

"Ohio."

Artis waited. She bit back the rush of words, all of it about to spill out. And he thrust his lip out, as though he'd been apprised of something, and turned to pay for his lumber order.

It wasn't until he left with a curt nod that she realized what had transpired. This was a place where stories were given, where people talked to strangers in the fields, where they offered intimacies about doctor visits and family trouble. And she had failed to tell her tale in return. A violation. *Shit.*

Tracey had made a real effort to be more open after that, had gone out of her way on the infrequent occasions they'd met. He was always smiling, stood a little closer than maybe he had to, seemed genuinely interested in what she was doing at the old farmhouse. And then she had so overreached. She saw him draw away, heard that last remark, "Too much cat in you for a hound like me."

The bell jolted her. The students filed out, sliding their papers onto her desk.

Second period, she had study hall.

Third period, she recited something about the Louisiana Purchase, something she'd just read or half remembered, and then handed out worksheets.

Fourth period, lunchroom duty. Dave wasn't at his usual post. Instead, Ray Koch teetered on his Hush Puppies and sucked in his cheeks and ignored her, as a guidance counselor and properly married Baptist deacon should.

When the bell rang at 11:50, she went up to the AV center and found Dave had already rolled out a TV on a cart, hooked it to the cable and tuned in Channel 6: "Our top story, authorities await the medical examiner's report in the tragic death of a Saul County schoolgirl."

Tracey sat down, the heavy wooden chair a comfort. The anchorwoman shuffled papers. An icon in the screen corner showed the chalk outline of a body, as though a murder had been discovered.

The report cut to the front of the courthouse, where the sheriff, a big man wearing a brown suit, stood dead center of the camera and looked worried. "We're waiting on the medical examiner's report," he said. "She was bit, there's no doubt, but we don't know what all happened out there."

"Have you located the dogs?" the reporter asked.

"We have not located the dogs. The owner of the dogs in question is said to be Mr. Pennell. He said his dogs sometimes take off after deer. We have not located any dogs that fit the description."

The camera cut away, to the reporter holding a mike in front of the Saul County Jail. "While a witness has identified dogs belonging to Artis Pennell as the culprits in this horrible death, Mr. Pennell said in an interview earlier today he doesn't believe his pets are to blame."

A momentary pause, the image flickered out, and then Artis was being interviewed. He was standing in front of the family home—she recognized that clutter of barns—shoulders uneven from one hand jammed in his jeans pocket, his ball cap tipped back as she was sure the cameraman had asked to eliminate the shadow. "Those dogs are my son's pets. They wouldn't attack a child," he said, his voice as level as his gaze—straight, it seemed, at her. "That woman said my dogs did it, but nobody else saw them. Who knows if it was even dogs? Maybe that poor little girl got hit by a car, or something."

"No," she whispered, as the broadcast moved on to other disasters. "No, I tried to scare them away."

Dave put his hand on her shoulder. She jumped, startled, and he moved away to turn off the television.

"I didn't say they were just his dogs. Two of his dogs," she said. "I know those dogs."

Dave pulled a chair over and sat down, hands hanging between his knees. "It sounds like it was a terrible night out there."

"Lakesha got off the bus. I saw the dogs running and called to her, but then they knocked her down." She tried to remember exactly how she had told the deputy. "I drove up the lane and honked and yelled and tried to scare them away. I couldn't see where she was. The dogs were all over. One tried to come into the car after me. I saw blood on them." She wasn't sure if her voice held out to say that aloud, or if she only thought the words.

"Did anyone else see it?"

The empty fields, empty road, dark trailers. "No," she whispered. "I drove to my house and called for help. When I got back the dogs were gone. Lakesha—I covered her up. In the ditch where I found her."

There was nothing more to say. Tracey felt the cold settle in her stomach, as it had last night, as she saw the dog fling the book bag aside and realized they were wild, blood-hungry, like wolves. When she couldn't get out of the car to help. When she was helpless, unable to save that child.

"Damn that Artis!" Dave pushed himself out of the chair and Tracey was amazed at the change in him, the way his jaw was set and his hands worked into fists and then opened, as though he were trying to calm a rage that threatened real harm. "What does he think he's doing, making accusations?"

"It's my word against his," she said, realizing it as she spoke it. The way the sun was disappearing in the clouds, the dogs running, Lakesha stumbling, and then she couldn't see her any more.

"No, it's not. The reports will show that. He should take the dogs out and shoot them and be done with it, before they tear up someone else."

She winced.

"Why would he even suggest such a thing?" he asked.

Tracey couldn't bring herself to tell him what had happened, why Artis might think she had it in for him. Her pride was still writhing on the pin he had stuck through it that day. She knew what people would say, a woman scorned, a woman scorned.

Those words mocked the click of her heels on the worn terrazzo, walking alone to her next class. Surely, she thought, it can't be worse than this morning. But she felt off-center and vulnerable as soon as the kids settled at their desks and sat, looking at her. Someone in the back rows burped, a prolonged belch that ripped the silence, and the laughter that followed was almost hysterical. She smiled it away instead of making it a discipline issue. Tracey smiled and smiled until the students were shamed into silence and she regained control of the classroom.

She moved through the lecture rapidly, skipping the subtleties, the opportunities for student-teacher interaction. She wrote key words on the blackboard, and a few students copied them down. Worksheets passed out, the assignment given for tomorrow. "Any questions?"

"I heard you found Lakesha."

Tracey looked up from her plan book. Shalynda, who held her head up, fearless when she stalked through the school on four-inch heels, who didn't back down from anyone, including the father who had been convicted of assaulting her.

"Yes," she said, standing, looking right back at her.

Shalynda shook her head and the red-tinted braids flew up and settled. "We hear the TV," she said. "We hear tell, maybe you done run over that child."

Tracey put both hands flat on the desk, and thought, this is the worst, the rumors fly so fast, they grow wings and maybe horns and tails.

"By accident," added Jorge. "Was it an accident, Miss Gaines?"

He had a tender heart, she thought. Who would have suspected?

"I saw Lakesha get attacked," she said, each word coming out individually like the name of some historic document. "I tried to get the dogs away from her, but I couldn't. I went to call for help and then I came back and tried to help her until the ambulance got there."

Her voice was hardly shaking at all, but she could hear one word, over and over. Tried. Tried.

Failed.

The class was quiet again, and stayed that way until dismissal. And that was the worst of it, no more questions, students from other classes picking up the eddying rumors and her answer as they crossed in the hall.

She saw to the bus loading and finally, bone-weary, went to her car. Two deep wavering lines had been dug into the paint on the driver's side, from the mirror all the way to the taillights, the deliberate keys cutting through the new scratches and old, through the dark gray, all the way to the bare metal.

CHAPTER FIVE

The directions seemed clear enough: Take Route 59 south to the intersection of Coswell Road and turn left. That will take you into Coswell community. The church is on the left.

Tracey drove through the crossroads that was Coswell, a blinking red light where another state route came slanting into the cluster of houses, churches and a convenience store/diner.

Word of God Holiness Church. Wesley Free Methodist Church. A tiny Episcopal chapel, wearing the certain elegance that even the poorest of them seemed to have. All were on the left-hand side, the first in a converted service station with the bay doors painted with crosses, the second built in block, the third in fieldstone. Mr. Arbogast had said the church was brick, and set back from the road.

The houses quickly thinned to farms. Tracey turned around in a driveway, between a pair of concrete flower baskets, and went back through Coswell at a crawl. Word of God, Wesley, Holy Trinity. She peered down the two-block side streets that ended at the railroad tracks. Her hands shook a little on the steering wheel. She would be late. Vibrating with too much coffee and not enough sleep, still she couldn't understand where she could have gone wrong. How could you lose a church in a place this small?

An old man was opening the door of a blue pickup in front of the diner. Tracey rolled her window down fast and shouted, before he could get inside, "Can you tell me where to find Mt. Zion Missionary Baptist Church?"

The man turned toward her, stiffly, planting one foot and then the other. "Mt. Zion?"

"Yes."

"That's a black church, ma'am."

"I know."

He took off his cap and ran his fingers through uncombed gray hair. "Well, then, at the fork here you bear left, and you'll see it after a space. It sets back."

"Thank you, sir," she said, honorifics somehow coming readily these days, his age demanding the word even as she pondered his comment. A black church, as though that made any difference, but of course it did. She pulled away, waiting for traffic to pass so she could cross. He didn't really seem racist about it, just making sure that she knew what she was looking for—but that in itself....

After about a half-mile, she spotted the low brick building, modest behind a grove of tall oaks that sheltered a graveyard. A wooden cross perched above the entryway. The church was on the right-hand side, however, and she wondered where Mr. Arbogast had been giving directions from.

Two black men in narrow black suits directed cars into a field growing up in grass that hid the ruts. She crept past the other cars and parked at the end of the row. Grass brushed against her ankles as she hiked back and she wondered if there could be chiggers this early, with the recent chill replaced by sudden warmth, the spring sun brighter than it should be. That old man. He hadn't said anything out of line, really, had said black instead of colored like some did. It was no different from in her old neighborhood, she thought. If a stranger asked for St. Paul's the first thing would be to ask, do you want the Methodists or the Lutherans?

Cars were still coming in. Out on the side of the road was a van from *NewsCenter 4*. The cameraman was set up to one side, filming the church. The other station must be here, too, and surely the newspaper reporters. They'd bothered her, calling for comments, then one by one giving up—all but a reporter from the county weekly.

She hadn't even gone inside when she first got home last night. Instead, she crouched on the porch steps, tempting Garland with the deli chicken left over from her untouched lunch. He was closer than he'd ever been, ready to take the morsel, when the phone rang and they both jumped. She ran to the kitchen, and the man's voice was familiar though she couldn't place it, a bland Midwestern accent that seemed almost welcome until she heard him say, "from *The News-Banner.*"

"Ms. Gaines," he persisted. "We'd like to get your response to Mr. Pennell's comments."

She didn't answer.

"Ms. Gaines? It's only right, for you to have your say. We always want to give both sides when an accusation ..." His voice trailed away as she lowered the receiver and felt the satisfying finality as it cradled on the black 1960s telephone.

Tracey walked into the library, where she'd had the phone company run a modern phone line that would connect to her computer and answering machine. The red message light reflected in the bare windows, 12, 12, 12. The messages had come the day after the death, the day when Artis Pennell said she lied, had even implied she had killed the girl. The calls she'd saved were mostly crisp journalistic voices asking for her comments, ones she'd left on the tape to stop any more. But there were others. Those she kept—just in case.

Tracey listened again.

"You ought to be ashamed, to lay the blame off on Mr. Pennell." The woman's voice shook. "This family's been here for generations, never would they allow such a thing."

Then Ellen Friedlander from school, offering sympathy.

"A real woman wouldn't of took off and left that girl to die."

And the worst, the one she couldn't listen to again, the one where she let go of the "play" button as though it were scalding hot, "Even a nigger child deserves better ...."

Through the evening the calls had continued, the old mechanical burr of the phone in the kitchen, the electronic ring in the den. Four rings, then the machine. She had sat in the kitchen, a cup of coffee cooling in her hands, waiting for each click like the loading of a gun, and her voice: "We're not at home right now. Please leave a message."

At the church door, an usher glanced at her and asked if she was from the school. She nodded. There looked to be no place to sit—the pews packed with women in hats, teenagers occupying the folding chairs against the walls and the family together up front, closest to the little white casket covered with a blanket of pink roses. Tracey saw Orenna huddled in the arms of an older man. Her father? She felt eyes on her, looking, sliding away, an obvious stranger; she knew no one and they couldn't know who she was. There were a couple of other white people here, but not from the school—and now she saw Mr. Arbogast, and Penny Miller who was Lakesha's teacher, and the elementary school secretary. Their pew was full. The usher guided Tracey, his hand positioned a finger's breadth from her arm, to a folding chair at the back.

Tracey crossed her ankles, started to settle back in the seat but heard the chair creak and decided it was wiser if not so comfortable to sit straight. She wished she'd come earlier, so she could be with the others. She had thought Dave might be here, although she hadn't asked. Until this morning she hadn't been at all sure that she would be here. Duck and cover, that was her response to trouble most times. But the voices on the telephone had steeled her. If she didn't come to the funeral, if she didn't claim her right to be there, then she might as well pack up and keep moving. The house, the cats, this refuge she was building board by board—she couldn't just leave. Again.

The church hummed with conversation, people who all seemed to know each other. The windows, squares of alternating blue and green stained glass, let in a little air though narrow tilt-outs at the bottom. She focused on the altar, the bare little stage for all this grief. The wall behind it had been painted with an incongruous image of a Teutonic Jesus, flowing blond hair and blue eyes and skin pale as a sacrificial lamb's. It was an old mural, cracked along one side where the wall had settled and the stucco parted along the seams. On the pulpit was a poster of an African Jesus—just as incongruous, she thought, to see the savior with dreadlocks, bare-chested under the red Masai robe slung off one shoulder.

She wished for one of the stick-handled fans that had materialized in the close air, like something out of an old movie. The women and old people fanned briskly, pictures of Dr. King and the rugged cross signaling, while the children swatted each other or sat with the fans limp in their hands.

The man beside Orenna stood up and Tracey realized it was the preacher; what she thought was a mourner's black suit was actually a robe with African weavings down the front, a multicolored field patterned with brown hands raised in supplication to the cross.

A voluminous woman sat down at an electronic organ and began to play, for a few minutes overlapping the taped music that someone finally thought to turn off. Tracey recognized a melody here and there. The congregation settled down, talk ebbing until there was just the whisper of fans in the space between notes. A side door creaked and the choir filed in, a billow of royal blue.

The service reminded her of her grandmother's Brethren church, the prayers long and the preacher passionate as he called on the name of Jesus. He paced from the pulpit to the organ and back. "This child is a lamb of God, yes, called by the Shepherd to come and lie down beside still waters ...."

"Yes, yes," the congregation said.

"Beside peaceful waters."

"Amen."

"Not a child in the county with a brighter smile, do you hear me?" He shook his head. "Not a child sweeter."

"Oh my soul," a woman called.

"She carried brightness with her everywhere, this child, this smiling child, yes, Lord," he said, and mopped his brow. The fans whispered. "Yet we wonder, Lord, why you called her home. Can we ask the Shepherd why? Can we now know that she was lifted out of her pain to be the very lamb in his holy arms. Lakesha Precious...."

The name sent a shock through her. Precious. The white coat swinging wide as she turned and smiled.

"She has been restored to perfection, rocked in the arms of Jesus, in the arms of Jesus Christ." A flower slipped from the blanket covering the casket, and the preacher lifted it high before the congregation, and there was nothing to say or to respond. Tracey felt the shuddering start in her throat, the weeping about to break out, and she bent her toes hard in her shoes until the pain held her sorrow back.

The choir sang, a tune that thumped along, "Keep your lamps trimmed and burning" three times before a soprano voice rose above the rest, "For your work is almost done." The song went on, the verses repeating and repeating, until the hypnotic rhythm insinuated the words into her consciousness. *For your work is almost done.*

The congregation stood in silence as four teenage boys, one of them in black sneakers, carried the casket from the altar to the hearse. Two others, not needed for such a small body, walked behind like outriders, their hands folded in front and heads bowed.

As the church doors opened, Tracey heard a car roar past, the muffler long gone, and in the silence after, a dog's bark.

The family followed the casket down the aisle. Orenna walked very straight beside the usher, with her baby asleep in the arms of a woman who from her round face must have been her sister, part of that train of aunts and uncles and nieces. Orenna pressed a lace-edged handkerchief to her eyes. Just as she passed the last pew Orenna lowered her hand, looked up with eyes that were beyond tears, straight into Tracey's face.

Misery made her eyes wide and dark as they'd been that night, pools of anguish. Dry and hot and deep, a night sky building a storm, and in the depths, a flash of righteous anger that sparked across the gap between them.

Tracey suddenly felt the sweating bulk of the man next to her, felt his hands grip her shoulders to steady her.

"I'm sorry," she said, "please excuse me for bumping into you," unable for a moment to realize how she had come to fall into his arms. She smoothed her dress, pulling herself together. What had happened? Orenna's eyes—she had physically flinched from that look.

She walked as quickly as decorum would allow, out of the church, away from the mourners, ignoring Mr. Arbogast's booming voice, "Ms. Gaines, Ms. Gaines," and she felt like a student caught in the act, guilty.

She stumbled back through the field, almost falling once, catching herself with a hand on the fender of a car, and then pulling her hand away as though burned, as though someone might shout in anger at her trespass.

The prayer cycled through her head, the one line so often said in a low mumble, "forgive us our trespasses." Now the words burned.

She had trespassed by what she hadn't done, by the cowardice that left the child to be torn and thrown aside in the ditch. In her car she kept the windows rolled up, muffled in heat and silence. The dove-gray hearse pulled out, followed by the funeral procession, blue flags on the fenders and headlights on. It was not a long procession.

All down the highway, Tracey saw how approaching cars pulled off to the side of the road and waited, doing what they could in respect, then gradually went on their way as the taillights faded.

CHAPTER SIX

It had seemed easier to talk about school, but the conversation had come to a stop right where Dave hoped it wouldn't—with the teachers, the gossip in the lounge. The whole sorry mess about Lakesha.

"See those greenhouses?" Tracey was staring out her window at a farm, the white plastic domes gleaming. "Tobacco. You need every day of growth you can get—more days, more leaf, more profit."

He saw how her eyes darted, absorbing the landscape, the fence-line trees, the soil tilled in strips between belts of alfalfa, the chinked-log barns reclining back toward the ground.

"It cost a lot to farm," he said, slowing for a red light holding up one other car at a crossroads in the middle of nowhere. "Greenhouses, curing units, seed—and now the buyers want the tobacco baled."

"Like hay?" Her interest was piqued.

He felt himself expounding but at least this was a safe topic. "The buyers demanded baled leaf, instead of loose, and so the farmers paid for that equipment. Now they're going to squeeze out the little guys, between imported leaf and contract buying."

"And the lawsuits, of course."

"That, too." She probably didn't hold with tobacco, he realized. It was a right hard thing to defend.

He didn't pick up the topic again, and neither did she. He wasn't bothered by the silence, still absorbing the reality of Tracey sitting beside him in the passenger seat, headed south to Raleigh for dinner.

He had asked and been surprised when she accepted his invitation, then wondered if she hadn't done so out of pure loneliness, brooding alone in that huge old house. In some way he felt he had taken advantage of her desperation.

Dave watched the traffic, most of it headed toward them, out of the city to the subdivisions rearing their gates beside the highway. He was too aware of her eyes, and how her movement had released a new burst of that green scent he'd noticed, not perfume, more like an herb garden in the sun. Rosemary and lavender. He remembered the scents of the knot garden behind his grandparents' home, the pots on his mother's windowsill. *Rosemary, that's for remembrance.*

"The first time I ever had Thai food was in New York," he offered. "I got something with coconut milk and fish and about couldn't get it down."

"I'm set for some pad Thai. I gotta tell you, I did a double-take when I saw a sushi bar down here. All sorts of stuff seeping into the South."

Seemed like all the newcomers were finding, to their amazement, that the South wasn't quite what they had imagined, plantation houses hidden behind live oaks or Mayberry and Andy Griffith or Daisy Duke. They ran smack up against RTP and biotechnology firms, Mexican tiendas and Jewish temples, I-40 and shopping malls so big they had to have not one but two Victoria's Secret stores.

"I guess I've gotten used to eating at home," she said, a conciliatory tone that said she knew she'd been snide. "By the time I get through at school, I'm just worn out. And the cats like company."

"How many cats do you have?" He held a momentary image of the crazy old woman who lived on Meredith Street when he was a kid, with newspapers and books filling every room of the big brick house where cats went in and out of broken windows. She weighed about 80 pounds but it took two deputies to carry her out, one under each scrawny arm. She went to a nursing home and the humane society had to euthanize all but a handful of the 93 cats.

"Six, now. They came with the place."

"The Langs must have left them," he said, remembering their blank-faced son, a serial shoplifter at 14, a sneak thief or arsonist in the making. The family was from somewhere over east. They moved in and moved back in the space of a year.

"They're pretty wild—maybe they were there before."

Dave missed the street he wanted and realized he must have let out some sort of noise because Tracey stopped talking and looked at him. He rolled his eyes, said he'd goofed and would have to make a go-around.

"Anyway," she said, "I started putting pans of food out for them, starved as they were. Old Garland was the first one to actually stick around when I opened the door—stood there and ate while I watched. He was really beat-up, his ear chewed."

"Aren't you afraid of rabies?"

"I trapped them and gave them shots."

Dave glanced at her, wondering how she managed that.

"It's not hard, you just back them up in the corner of the Hav-a-Heart with a heavy blanket and stick the needle in."

"Not much different from teaching, then?"

"Given the day, given the day!"

She rattled around in her purse and came out with a small flat tin of something, lip gloss. The traffic light was red, shining through the windshield, and he watched her run her finger over her lips, without a mirror. A car honked behind him and he saw the left arrow had turned green, hit the gas and made the turn to park behind Thai Garden.

"I just love the old place, you know?" Tracey clicked the tin and dropped in back in her purse. "The first time I saw that house, I was done for, and the real estate agent knew it. I walked the boundaries but didn't really care what was out there—the house was what I wanted—but I've been exploring. I found a family graveyard, old roads."

"It has a tale or two, that place. Remind me to show you in the *Saul County History*," he said as they got out. He regretted it immediately. If she ever opened that big green book she'd see it was written by a Fordham (his uncle Lindsey), and notice the embarrassing number of pages devoted to his family tree.

"There's even a patch of big woods that might be virgin forest, huge old oaks." She was standing on the other side of the car, and she threw her hands up in a double arc to show how tall, how wide the old trees were, her face now lit up. He smiled, too, catching that brighter mood and hanging on.

She was quickly ahead of him, already inside the double doors and being greeted by the elderly host when Dave humped up beside her. "Two, please—nonsmoking," she said, and her voice was cool and businesslike, the enthusiasm locked away.

They followed the man, whose turquoise sneakers seemed apt with his floral-print shirt, over a tiny arched bridge. Water cascaded from a fountain by the bar, trickled and fell over rocks and disappeared into a koi pool near where they were bowed to a table.

Tracey appeared to be a city girl at ease back in the city—but also, it seemed to Dave, elusive, seeming to withdraw into the dark tangle of foliage that surrounded the pool. She was strong but quick to retreat, like one of her cats that when wounded would seek a thicket. This whole thing now, Lakesha's death—he'd heard the talk, and knew she must have as well, filtered through the school. How there must have been more to it, those dogs just coming out of nowhere, never done a thing, and this girl dead. And there were the ones who would have jumped out of the car and beaten the dogs back with their bare hands, but it was all false bravado. She did what she could do, what most of them really would have done.

Dave counted his breaths, three, four, let it all go away—this was nothing that he wanted to think about now or let her guess that he was thinking.

He had forgotten this was so intimate a place, the water burbling, orchids draping from above—artificial, but pretty—and couples everywhere. Tracey glanced over the top of her menu, her eyes bright, and he felt, well, yes, as if it were a date. It could be, though he hadn't called it that.

He wasn't sure what to say.

"The specials look good," she said.

"Yes, I saw that." Dave plunged into the menu. *Don't get the cart before the horse.*

When he'd come back to North Carolina, he didn't have much in the way of expectations. There was his mother, of course. He rented his own place, one side of a former millworkers' duplex, got a new card at the Shawton Library where he'd borrowed books since he could walk, bought a couch and a TV and a satellite dish. He knew what to expect. These little towns, scattered around the county, faded from their prosperous years in textiles and tobacco, were places people left on Friday nights looking for fun. The girls married young and settled down to raise kids, and the biggest social event from week to week was the local high school football game.

After a year or so, he found himself caught between loneliness and inertia. He went to Durham and Raleigh a few times, felt old and bald at the bars, felt obviously alone and trolling at the museums. Lately, lured by the ads when he checked his e-mail, he'd been touring the dating sites on the Internet, looking at the electronic profiles of unobtainable women seeking men. Sometimes he thought about paying the membership so he could contact them, but wondered what would he say? "Follically challenged educator in search of a soul mate .... likes books, old movies, nights by the fireplace, walks on the beach—those would be slow walks since he's half crippled."

He realized that Tracey was looking at him. Had he made a noise again, was he talking to himself? That's what came of living alone. Dave felt a blush headed up his cheeks and was mortified. At least he was sitting down, his leg as good as anyone's now.

"I wonder where that waiter got off to?"

"They don't seem to be in a hurry. But that's OK," she said.

"Would you like to share an appetizer? Most of them are pretty big—for one. A lot of couples come here from out in the country. It's not like there's a place to eat up there, for a date, I mean, not like the barbecue for lunch," Dave said, hearing one wrong thing after another coming out of his mouth.

Tracey nodded. "There isn't even a decent movie theater. I didn't realize what it was like. I came in through Raleigh-Durham and thought, well, this won't be so far away, but it's like forever at the end of a day. And if you stay there in the county, well," she ended with a sniff.

"Small towns."

"And everybody's been there forever, and has been married forever. There's not a smidgen of social life. The teachers are all married and they don't include singles in their parties. Odd numbers and all that."

"I guess they expect you'll go to church," he said, half teasing.

"Oh, yeah. Ray Koch and his hand-wringing. Every time he gets around me he starts that, like I'm going to jump on him or something." He saw her look up, bite her lip, and realized the waiter was standing silently behind him.

Tracey ordered a salad with peanut dressing and something unfamiliar from deep in the menu. Dave fell back on the spring roll and special number two.

"I don't mean to bitch," she said, the word startling him a bit. "It's tough starting out anywhere. I wanted to come South, wanted the nice weather and the flowers. I wanted to get away from the godforsaken snowbelt and did I ever."

He felt the pang of isolation, how alone she must feel, and wanted to tell her it was no better for a hometown boy. Single was single, alone was alone, it didn't much matter. Except that people in your own town knew that you were alone, and why.

"Why are you at the alternative school? You're too good a teacher." Her sudden head-cocked curiosity cut off any commiseration. She sipped at her water and waited for his answer like an opponent across the chessboard.

"You know I'm from here, originally."

"From Saul County."

"My family goes all the way back on both sides. The Old North State and all that. Revolutionary War, Civil War."

Tracey's mouth curled at the corners. "I thought you called it the War of Northern Aggression, or the Troubles."

"That's Ireland," he jabbed. "Might that red in your hair betray a touch of Irish?"

"Hah!" She sat back and her hair swung. "Could be from a bottle, you know. But yes, Irish, really Scots-Irish. And Czech."

"German and English, here. On my mother's side, some of the first people to come inland from the coast. There's a little crossroads place in Pelham County, one over from here, that's named for my mother's mother's side. Littlejohn. That was the fighting side. Some of them were at the Battle of Moore's Creek, where they stopped the Loyalists."

Tracey nodded, but her face had the flat expression of students in his class. She might be a history teacher, but the Revolutionary War in the South was nothing that they taught in Ohio, it seemed.

"My father's people, though, came down from Pennsylvania, Quakers and Mennonites."

"Pacifists."

"Yes, but it wore off." Dave laughed. "My granddad was in the Navy, drafted, and my Dad signed up to see the world."

"Vietnam?"

"The Far East, but mostly the Philippines, Japan. Thailand." Dave watched as the old waiter set out their meals with soft deference, bowing his way back from the table in what seemed almost a parody. His father had written home from ports in Southeast Asia, letters that Dave had found later in a trunk. There were exotic stamps and papers, photographs of temples beside brown waterways, of smiling young girls in silk dresses, bright green paddy fields. A faded red tassel that fell from a card painted with birds. When he took these treasures to his mother to show her what he had found, she got angry and ordered it all put back. It was one of those family things; no one talked about his father's service, because his mother would lash out or turn away. It was years before he pieced it all together from the stray words of aunts and cousins. His father, married and later with Dave in diapers back in North Carolina, had prowled the bars of Manila and Bangkok, and nearly left his family over a passion for a teenage Filipina. As he had gotten older, and the letters in the trunk took on a mythic dimension, Dave tried to remember if his father had written about the girl. He sure had never spoken of her, nor did he ever talk about the Far East or the ocean or anything of what had lured and nearly held him.

"Anyway, he came home, and took up the family tobacco allotment. I was old enough to help out, eight or nine. Planting, chopping weeds. That first year I spent too long in the fields, priming, and got sick." He saw the flicker of incomprehension cross Tracey's face. "Priming is when you pull the lowest leaves off the plant, the ones with mud and dirt on them. Whenever you pull—that's how you say pick—tobacco, you get that nicotine sap on your skin, and it makes a lot of people puke."

"Lovely." She had a wry little dimple that appeared when she half-smiled, an apostrophe forming beside her mouth.

"It's hard work, tobacco. Used to be a lot of money in it, though, when families took care of their own fields. Today mostly it's Hispanic labor. They'll do the stuff our own kids won't do any more, pick strawberries or prime tobacco or work in the chicken farms."

"But you don't have the farm now."

He shook his head. "Dad gave it up. Said there wasn't a future in it. A lot of folks thought he was crazy. He went into sales."

Tracey pushed a long strand of vegetable aside on her plate. She handled the chopsticks elegantly, her long fingers stretched along the wood and carrying through the motion.

"Your mother?"

"She's passed on, too," he said. "Two years ago, come this winter." A brief still image came and went, a photo of his father and mother on their wedding day, holding hands but leaning away from each other. "No brothers or sisters."

They ate in silence. He pushed the bamboo shoots to the top of his plate, and Tracey reached across with the chopsticks and bore them away. She grinned when he followed her motion, at first rakishly, then the smile fading into insecurity. When at last she spoke, Tracey's voice was distant as though she had been called from some faraway place. "My parents still live in Ohio. My brothers—two— and their families live close by. I'm the one who cut and ran—as far as Cleveland, then Pennsylvania after we were married. And then when the marriage broke up, it just wasn't comfortable at the family gatherings anymore." Her voice sank, then she smiled with her lips pressed together, and began again. "I decided it was time to get out of the snow."

"Maybe you meant to move to Florida."

"Too far. I can get home in a day, if I have to. And we don't get enough snow to have to shovel it."

Dave remembered the absolute joy of snow, when enough fell at one time to allow for snowmen and sledding.

"You know, the prettiest thing I ever saw was snow," he said. "It was a little park in Baltimore, just after a heavy snow that kept people inside. It was like those photographs of Central Park in snow, pure white, the iron railings and the benches, and there was one old guy in a black topcoat walking a dog. White and black, and a little oval of blue sky where the storm was clearing."

"Well, I've shoveled enough for a lifetime," Tracey said. "When I came down to interview, the azaleas were in bloom and it was heaven."

He saw her raise her hand, open her mouth as if to speak, and he turned to see Marian Eddy and her mother. Marian, who ran the Quik-Mart not far from the school, nodded and said "good evening" to him as she passed, steadying her mother's uneven steps, but it was clear that she wasn't acknowledging Tracey.

Dave waited for Marian to turn back, to slap her forehead and say how she was getting senile, just didn't recognize Miz Tracey sitting there, but Marian kept walking and he couldn't make up a reason that he could get his mouth around. Short and sweet, he was ashamed.

Tracey's face was red. She set her chopsticks neatly down across the last of her meal. "I'm ready to go," she said, her voice just as controlled.

"I'm sure Marian just didn't recognize you."

She gave him a withering look and he didn't try any other excuses.

"I'll get the check," he said, looking around for the waiter, seeing no one. They went to the front and Tracey stood staring out the glass door while he got the bill paid and took a handful of mints, and caught the door as it swung back with Tracey's exit.

They headed back out of town, past the strip malls and the clusters of gas stations, out into the residential district where the lights were less frequent.

"I always believed that Southerners were friendly," she said at last. "People in Ohio, they're just cold. I came down here and everyone waved at me, I was driving through the country and people waved. I thought they mistook me for someone, but then I realized they just saw another human being. People up North look through you, most of the time."

He thought about Marian doing exactly that. And how Tracey had crumpled at the slight, then pulled herself back together.

"People talked to me in the stores, told me stuff about their families and their personal lives. But it's all skin deep. They don't really let you get close. It's phony."

Dave listened as if he were juggling china, as if a moment's inattention would let everything crash. "It just takes time to get to know people's way," he said.

"Superficial. Smiles that don't mean anything." She didn't even sound upset, just resigned, as though this was the culmination of all she'd come to expect.

"No, it's not that." He heard her heavy exhalation, saw how she crossed her arms on her chest. "We're taught to be nice. It makes things easier if there's some courtesy, even between strangers."

"So how do you know who you can trust to be your friend and who's just being *courteous?*"

Dave heard the sarcasm and wanted to counter that it wasn't like that. You know your own, your circle of friends, and caught himself as he realized that for Tracey, there was no core of people to rely on. No relatives or old neighbors or school chums. And now this thing with Lakesha.

In the blessed darkness, Dave reached over to touch her hand, still clenched around her other arm as she hugged her pain. He glanced from the road again, saw how her chin trembled.

"You weren't wrong to come here," he said. "It takes time in any new place. I've moved and sat alone in my apartment, someplace where I didn't know anyone. I've done the same thing right here. People like you, Tracey, but they don't know you yet. So Lakesha— it's only that ...."

"That I'm a Yankee bitch."

He didn't know what to say.

"When you taught up North," she began, her voice less sharp, and stopped. She was facing forward now, no longer turned away to the window and the outside. The glow from the dash was cool. "Was it so hard, when you went there?"

It was only her unshielded pain that allowed him to start talking about his own.

"I had lived all my life within 75 miles of home," he said. "Went to Chapel Hill. Student teaching in Durham, inner city. I started to think I could save the world, so I went to Baltimore to teach. A lockdown school."

He waited for the light to change before starting again.

"I thought I knew black people, because I grew up with them here, taught them, worked with them. But it was different in Baltimore. Not just them, everyone. Cold, you said. And hard." He felt the scald of shame, how his fear flooded through him, and he thought he would explode if he didn't tell her. "I'm afraid now. Afraid of them. The black students in my class, the way they look and sound now. Like the ones in Baltimore."

Tracey shifted in her seat, turning toward him. He saw her intent expression, that hunger to know, and he was ashamed, so ashamed.

"What happened, Dave?"

The sound of his name, said gently, made him want to cry. He felt how close he was to confession.

He shook his head. "I don't believe I want to talk more about it."

"You don't have to if you don't want."

"There was an—incident."

Tracey leaned toward him, intent, and he knew he must only have whispered. She was so close. If he told her the rest she would be embarrassed for him, would turn away from him. He left his hand loose on the console between them. He wanted her to take his hand, and then he could tell her everything. The past and the present tumbled through his thoughts, and his hand lay open, and she sat motionless as they crossed the Saul County line.

CHAPTER SEVEN

Tracey struggled to get the outside window all the way up along its groove, then the inside one down so she could clean it. Combination windows, the latest thing in the '50s. Dead bugs and leaves had to be routed out of the tracks with a screwdriver. As soon as she had the money, she would get all these replaced.

She spritzed the panes and wiped them clean. The glass stayed streaky. Years of oil heat had left a slick residue. Before that, coal. Fine black soot came from behind the baseboards, and the basement ended in a dank hole like the socket of a pulled tooth, the coal bin that once fed the furnace. She wondered how anyone ever stayed warm in this shell of a house, the walls a sandwich of horsehair plaster, wood, and clapboard, without insulation. Last winter brought a cold spell, a real Alberta Clipper. The janitor at school told her it was the coldest he ever remembered, "Right like one when I was a boy and they skated on the pond," he said. Tracey woke one morning to find snow sifted in through the bedroom windows. She had closed off the upstairs and slept in the small room off the kitchen.

She climbed off the chair to go clean the outside of the exposed pane. From the cedar tree, a bird sang, three times. The song changed and changed again. Mockingbird. Tracey couldn't identify most of the birds in her yard, or their songs, but the mocker she loved, standing spread-legged and tail-cocked on the fence, a delinquent with stolen songs. It sang on, louder than anything else, and she wondered if the birds were nesting yet.

Soon it would be spring break, but not soon enough. Except for Dave, sweet staunch Dave, the teachers pretty much treated her with the distant respect allowed to divorced women and lepers. The death of Lakesha and the nagging battle with Artis, carried on at third-hand through comments overheard or letters to the editor, hung around her. She was unlucky, a jonah, a carrier of a dangerous taint. Once she had read how the ancient Norse believed in numerous categories of luck, how you might have iron-luck and be able to smith tools, but not have fishing-luck, or woman-luck, or weather-luck. We haven't come so far, Tracey decided. Married women kept their men away from the divorcee, singles weren't invited over by couples, lest the mischance of a divorce drive away their marriage-luck. She had grown used to that kind of distance but not the general isolation that had followed the dog mauling.

Tracey rubbed dirt and sweat from her face with the back of her arm. The mockingbird had flown. Maybe she would blow money on a budget package to Cozumel or Aruba or some such place. The warm air nourished that wild-goose impulse.

She went back inside, lowered the screen, moved to the next window.

Tracey wondered about the traveling salesman who sold someone on this idea. A go-getter with a palette of aluminum siding samples and models of patent windows, now gone like the brush salesman and the vacuum cleaner salesman and even the Avon lady. No one stayed at home any more. No one came down the muddy roads to break housewives' long days for the price of a broom or a bottle of cake flavoring.

She pushed the inside window up and cleaned the exposed glass. It must have been difficult to get some old farm family to part with the dollars. Maybe the sheer sight of these dozens of windows had emboldened the salesman. What a coup!

It seemed she heard a knock at the front door. Too much thinking about old-time salesmen with their patter and their worn-out cars. Her grandfather had been such a salesman, but she didn't remember much but his big leather-covered sample case that stood by the hall tree. She spritzed and wiped and raised and lowered, picked up her bucket and Windex and squeezed the paper towel roll under her arm as she headed back outside.

Tracey banged back the screen door to see a skinny young man standing off to the side. He jumped, too, and looked flustered, turning away as through ready to run and then turning back to her.

"Hi," he said. "Hi, I'm Michael Keener."

Michael, she thought, not Mike. He was wearing a tie. A cheap tie.

She held the bucket of gray water in front of her. "Can I help you?"

He looked down as though trying to remember something, then met her eyes and said he was a reporter from the *Saul Citizen* (now the name was familiar) and wanted to ask for a few minutes of her time.

Tracey set the bucket down. A reporter. He rustled in the pockets of his oversized jacket. *I could knock him over with a feather.* So much for the cocky, aggressive journalist. She remembered the calls from the *News-Banner*, the larger newspaper from the city to the west. Keener had called too, insistent.

"Even if you hadn't caught me cleaning, I don't think I want to speak with you, Mr. Keener."

"Ms. Gaines ..."

"Please."

"Ms. Gaines, I have news."

"Yeah, I suppose you do," she said, laughing at the strangeness of it all. His white Cavalier sat in the drive, worn like a salesman's work car, a dent rusting into the near front fender.

"About the autopsy," he said firmly. He didn't have a local accent.

Tracey hesitated. "Have a seat," she said, nodding toward the bare metal of the cushionless glider. "I'll be out in a minute."

She set the bucket by the sink and washed and dried her hands. The breeze pulled the cotton curtains against the screen and puffed them out. Tracey lingered, rubbing lotion on her raw hands. What would she be asked to give up in exchange for this news? She decided to offer nothing.

She took the chair opposite and waited. Keener had a spiral-bound steno pad in his hand. Tracey wondered what secrets and embarrassments were already written there. The weekly printed them all, no crime too petty to be recorded, right down to a pack of cigarettes taken from a car.

"It's been a long time," he started. "I couldn't imagine why it took this long for the medical examiner's report."

She nodded. Not a word from her, nothing to add to this horror. She saw the dogs running again, saw Lakesha go down. Saw Lakesha's mother wailing, her mother's eyes nailing her to the wall in church, accusing her, accusing her.

"Dr. Beuerlein verified what you said. Lakesha Sipe died from loss of blood as a result of the dog bites. Nothing else. No other trauma evident but that caused by the dogs, he wrote."

Tracey stared past him at the twin camellias blooming by the path. Lipstick pink and white, they had seemed too bright just a day ago, too cheerful. Now the color matched her lifting spirits.

"You'll be putting that in the paper?"

He nodded enthusiastically.

"That's it, then?" she asked.

"Well, it's not all settled yet." His voice was very low. "The ME says the bite marks on Lakesha can't be matched to any particular dog. Some of them are the right size, but there was so much damage, and with several dogs involved—he said he can't match a specific dog to the attack."

She waited.

"Those dogs they picked up, Artis Pennell's dogs, are still at the county pound," he said.

"They'll destroy them, right?"

"Artis wants his dogs back," Keener said, then paused. "And an apology."

"An apology!" Her hands tingled with the flash of anger.

"He said …" Keener stopped, flipped the pages back in his notebook and read, "My boy has been hurt by all this. Jimmy wants his pets back. The ME said he doesn't know what dogs did this, and I don't believe they were mine. She owes us an apology for putting us through—through this and we need to get our dogs back." Kenner flopped the book forward, the pages fluttering closed under the weight of the cover. His pale brown eyes fixed on her, uncomfortably like a predator's, yet strangely vulnerable, needing her response.

"And I suppose the good ol' sheriff will do it," she said, at the same time remembering she had vowed to say nothing. Sheriff

Huck Webb was running for office yet again, at every crossroads a campaign sign with a masked crook caught in a red-and-blue web.

"I don't think so. Too many people are fired up about this," Keener said. "Did you read my piece about the drive to strengthen the leash law?"

Tracey felt him seeking approval, so much like a student lifting hopeful eyes as he set a book report on her desk. She kept her smile hidden. "I saw the story," she said. "The man with the beagles was fighting it."

Keener smiled broadly, showing uneven teeth. "That's it. But the leash law group, they're pretty organized. I think they're close to the number of signatures they need."

Tracey nodded. The reporter seemed to nod slightly in return, an echo or an encouragement.

"So you came all the way out here to tell me about the autopsy," she said at last. "I'd have thought the deputies would do that."

"I came all the way out here to get a comment," he said.

"On what?"

"On the findings."

"What do you want me to say, that I'm relieved? That doesn't bring back Lakesha."

He flipped the book open and began to write. Tracey put her hand on his wrist, halting him. A vein beat in the thin flesh. Startled, she pulled away.

"Don't add fuel to the fire," she said, aware how close she was to the edge of pleading.

The reporter sat motionless, pen poised.

"I'll say … let me say." Tracey stopped and closed her eyes. "I hope the report brings some closure for the family and community. Knowing that nothing will make the loss of Lakesha any less painful."

She started to cry, sadness chased by anger at her weakness, the tears hotter for that. She turned away and wiped her eyes.

Keener stood up, the porch glider squealing on its rusty runners. "I'm sorry to have upset you," he said.

She shook her head. "No, no. I appreciate that you brought me the information."

"I thought you'd want to know."

Tracey kept her head down, not wanting to start up again by looking at him and seeing concern, pity, whatever was there.

"I won't put in anything that would embarrass you," he said at last. "Good afternoon, Ms. Gaines."

She heard him walk down the steps, looked up in time to see a cat burst from under his car and streak across his path, headed for the shelter of the old chicken coop. Keener did a high step, stuttering to a stop while he looked around for more animals. Tracey laughed at his awkwardness, holding her hand over her mouth.

"I'm sorry, Mr. Keener," she said. "They're still wild."

"Call me Mike."

"Mike. OK. I'm Tracey. And Mike—thanks."

He raised his hand and got in the car, turned around and was gone.

Tracey sat for a while, as the momentary humor faded and she moved back through anger and surprise—an apology. *Good God.*

She called Garland, making the squeaking mouse sounds that always attracted his attention. He poked his head out from under the coop and made the interrogative meow that asked for food.

"Not right now," she said.

The black-and-white cat waited a moment more, then carried himself away proudly, tail high, as though there had been no stranger, no startlement, no refused request.

Tracey pushed herself to her feet, feeling the soreness in her calves from climbing up and down. She went in and picked up her bucket, but the water was cold and greasy and gray, and she was impatient at the thought of more window-washing. She wrung out the rag and threw it away, poured the water down the sink and chased it with scalding hot tap water.

Loose ends, she thought. It was all loose ends. She paused by the old telephone in the kitchen and picked up the heavy handset. The tone sounded distant. She started to dial her old number, Carl's number, but stopped after the area code. The dial spun back to stop. That wasn't a loose end, but something well tied up and done. The fullness in her chest got worse as she thought of their polite ending, the division of property, the love faded on his side but not so neatly on hers. Or the need for his friendship, his steady dark-toned voice if she called him now and asked what he thought.

Her loneliness would pour through the conversation, and she couldn't bring herself to admit that.

Maybe she would just call Dave and ask him to have dinner again. That had been a good night, all in all. She held down the buttons to get the tone back but after a moment set the handset back in the cradle. Why complicate things?

CHAPTER EIGHT

The wind had come up that fast, carried on the green edge of a front. She had been deep in grading papers and never heard it. It had been far too warm today; she'd noted the sun on her neck and the sweat under her breasts as she pruned the roses. Now her scratched arms ached and blisters burned, and the milky sky was disappearing under clouds the color of a bruise.

Tracey jumped when the screen door slammed against the outside wall. As she ran into the kitchen she saw it easing back, the metal pinging as the stretched spring relaxed, but another gust pulled it away from her hand and it slapped against the wall again. She caught hold of the handle and pulled it shut, hooked the latch down.

She loved storms but this kind scared her, out of sorts, out of season. Evening was coming on and the winds should be quieting, not whipping the tops of old trees back and forth. Back in Ohio, they'd be watching the TV, the reassurance of the weather radar showing yellow and orange, the blinking red centers of swirling winds. The older folks didn't trust such displays, but turned their black-and-white TVs all the way to black, and watched for the white bands of interference that screamed tornado and sent them to the cellars.

Hail or hard rain hammered on the tin roof. The driveway sizzled with the drops.

Tracey went back to the sofa, feet curled under her, the essays piled left and right as she read them and assigned grades. Though the wind whined in the attic and lightning shuttered across the wall, she refused to go to the damp basement and huddle.

How vulnerable you are in the country. The lack of street lights and close neighbors, no one to count on but yourself. Her grandmother shouting up the stairs, "Come run water, Tracey Ann. Storm coming." And the band of clouds rolling across the cornfields, her grandmother yanking screens out of windows and slamming them shut, and she would be running water in the bathtub and standing on tiptoes to reach the faucets in the kitchen sink and fill every pot and kettle. All her Grandmother Flora's hard work and preparation, the freezer full and the basement shelves stocked, wood piled, snow fence in place before Halloween—and she died anyway, died of cancer.

Tracey jumped up and moved through the house, living room to parlor to kitchen, looking out at the rain sheeting off the roof. Past the shelter of the porch, she could see red mud washing from her weeded beds, bleeding along the flagstones. Thunder rattled the old place. Tracey wished she'd been less stubborn and bought a TV, though what difference it made to know if there was a tornado watch or a tornado warning didn't seem clear.

"Why's a divorce and a tornado alike in West Virginia?" she remembered the joke Ohioans told. "Either ways you lose the trailer."

Lightning, thunder, more rain. It surged like surf. The lights flickered. Tracey took the oil lamp from the sideboard and lifted off the fragile chimney, lighted it, turned down the smoking wick until it gave a steady glow. She lit candles in their tall crystal holders on each side of the mantle in the parlor. The worn mirror reflected the flames as though seen through a sheer curtain. Another flicker, and a surge, the bulbs flaring with too much electricity, and then abruptly the power was gone.

The computer screen was blank, the ever-blinking light of the answering machine was dark. No sounds of refrigerator compressor or water pump or fan. But the house was more alive in some ways, the flames moving and casting shadows, the roof clamoring and the whole place aware of its joints. Finally she settled at the enamel-topped kitchen table, opened the drawer on the side and pulled out her project folder. The oil lamp was good enough to read by now as it had been a hundred years ago. She pulled out the kitchen redesigns. Sketches for expanding the bathroom. A rose arbor she liked, the page surreptitiously pulled out of a magazine in the dentist's office. There was so much she could do here, though sometimes she wondered if she wasn't overdoing it, like the nights she cooked salmon and risotto and fresh peas only to eat alone.

She flipped through design books from the Home Depot. She was drawn to kitchens like ones she remembered from Ohio, but then found them too white, the spaces too open. Flip, flip, flip. She realized that she was paging in time to music.

The storm was past. It was pitch black, except through the trees where light showed in the trailer park. A strong, pulsing melody rose from the same area. But this road was all on the same circuit.

She walked out, the night warm and still, water dripping off the porch roof and thunder grumbling far away as the storm raced east. She breathed in the rich mucky smell of mud and roots and exposed soft creatures. Her eyes adjusted and she picked her way across the yard, the stones pale amidst the grass. She moved toward the dark edge of her property, a belt of longleaf pines that gave off a sharp scent of resin. The lights came clearer. Underfoot, her stride was cushioned as she crossed years of fallen pine needles.

Beyond the waste ground, along the sketchy road, six trailers. The one where Lakesha and her mother had lived was empty now; according to last reports, Orenna Sipe and her baby had moved in with her sister across the line in Blossom County. Tracey looked away from that empty ache to where the light blared, and the music. One of the trailers occupied by migrant workers had a generator chugging away on the back of a pickup truck, its beat coming through the gap of the music and showing in the pulse of the patio lights strung in two directions. Two other trucks were turned toward that trailer, their headlights crossing in its yard like movie kliegs.

"*Vayamos, vayamos!*"

Women's laughter. Three men stood by the trucks and two women. There was a rapid exchange of Spanish, a word here and there that she understood. The music stopped and then started again, a sweet pair of voices raised over accordion, guitars, and drums.

A young woman in a dress with a narrow waist and full skirt

came out of the trailer. A man came to the tiny porch and held his hand up to her. She shook her head. He nodded, emphatically, and his fingers parted. The woman put her hand in his and the others cheered as he led her like a princess down the steps into the full glare of the headlights. The man gathered her in his arms and whirled her around, her skirt flaring and his white T-shirt aglow.

Tracey's heart swelled. Carl had lifted her like that. They were on spring break from college. Ocean breezes gusted up the boardwalk and billowed the blue peasant skirt above her head. The whistles. Carl's deep laughter, calling her Marilyn. She held the skirt down with both hands then, her pocketbook strategically positioned, until a little kid who had been eyeing them came up and pulled at her hand. "Hey," he whispered. "If you need to go to the bathroom, I know where they are."

A second couple began to dance, while the others stood around and clapped and whistled. The music slowed and the couples swayed closer together. Tracey watched for a little while more, feeling only gratitude that she'd been offered this glimpse.

She went upstairs to bed. The small light of the turned-down oil lamp reflected in the glass and gilt frames of photographs on the wall, but she could not see faces. The music pulsed. Tracey turned over and pushed her head deep into the pillow. The young woman spun in the man's arms, his black hair gleaming. At the end of the dance, he had bent his head and kissed her, and she curved gently back against his arm.

She hoped they fell in love and got married and raised a houseful of kids. Maybe if she and Carl could have had kids, it would have made a difference. Oh, but what happened between them had nothing to do with family, only with the discovery that their affection was more friendship than love. She refused to be bitter. Carl had been as kind and considerate as he could be, parting from her, untwining their lives. Too many women were angry and carried that lead weight around as if it was a right rather than a burden. Just yesterday morning, she'd been listening to Olivia Quarles in the lounge. "I told my daughter, lock me up if I ever think about getting serious with a man again," she said.

"I don't know." Tracey looked down into her empty cup, coffee stain webbing the china. "I like being on my own. It's taught me a lot about myself. But when the time comes, I'd like to find someone."

Olivia gave a sharp "huh" and followed it with her analysis of men, not one in a thousand of them mature the day they died, ruled by their senses but blind to emotional needs. "Grubs, they're all grubs." Tracey had to get up and leave.

She thought of Carl and wished there had been some other way. He used to pick dandelions early in the morning and shake the pollen from them across her face while she still slept. She woke with yellow stippling her cheeks like a child playing at Indian.

Tracey rolled over. Carl was teaching at the community college back in Pennsylvania, still living in their old house. Walking through the same dandelions on the scruffy lawn.

Maybe she should get out of public schools. A community college, perhaps, or one of the private academies. But she didn't like the kind of people who put their kids in the academies to get away from poor kids, black kids. Kids like Lakesha. She remembered the shy smile when she tried on the new coat and ran her fingers over the bright blue zippers. Her coat flying open, running, her white coat flying open.

Stop it, she told herself. The counselor had told her she could quiet such spinning thoughts, assign a time for worry and keep it there. I cannot do anything about these matters tonight, she told herself firmly. I will consider them tomorrow morning, on the drive to school. I will consider them tomorrow morning and not until then. She did deep breathing, counting her breaths in and out, her body rising and falling in a slow rhythm.

* * * * *

Tracey sat straight up in bed, heart pounding.

Her head was filled with the smell of smoke, the sound of men shouting, the heat of flames.

A dream—a nightmare—her house was barricaded, the whole place wrapped in barbed wire. Over the doors, the windows, a net of bright steel points. People screamed and shook their fists. And then there was fire. Yellow fire set at the corners of the house, on the porch, at the doors. She was trapped in the burning house, the smoke billowing, the heat.

Tracey shuddered. The oil lamp had gone out but the room was full of light, the moon shining in from a clear sky. But the shouting—that was real. Men arguing.

She pulled the quilts up and wrapped herself in them, cold from the sweat standing out on her skin, then clammy from the sweat in the sheets. The men's voices were too muffled to hear words, but she recognized the inflection as Spanish, and realized the shouting came from the trailer park road, close to where she had stood to watch the dancing.

Quiet again, then the sound of a truck roaring away. And then quiet.

Tracey huddled in the damp bedclothes, shaken by the vivid dream and irritated at her fearfulness.

When Carl had gone and she was alone, she wallowed in small fears. None of them was worth her waking nights, but she couldn't get out of that morass. She was never a daring child, and adulthood had made her more timid. The divorce gutted her confidence. Back then she would hear sounds in the night and stay awake, angry at herself in just the same way. How had she let herself fall into that, into that woman-alone stereotype?

Once she had driven past a gun show and then gone back, thinking she might just get a gun. She wandered through the booths, the camouflage outfits, Nazi memorabilia, the guns in rows and racks, the targets and bullets and paraphernalia she couldn't name, and it seemed there wasn't another woman in the place except for an Annie Oakley sort doing trick shots on the stage at the end of the hall. Nothing to give her security, there or anywhere. As the marriage ended, one insecurity piled on another, and anxiety clenched her chest and burned in her stomach. The prescription had numbed it but not made it go away. Nothing did, not the meetings with lawyers or even the divorce papers in her hand, not until Carl called one day to ask if he could come collect his high school diploma, forgotten in the bookcase, and she said yes. She cleaned up the place for his visit, because they were still friends of course, but when he came he stood at the bottom of the steps and said he didn't think he should come in—could she get it? She set the blue leatherette folder his hand and he said thank you. That was when the insecurity ended and the pure, plain loneliness began.

Her thoughts swirled like blackbirds over the fields, rising and falling to disappear on the ground, whirling up in a black funnel. Emptiness pulling her thoughts into a spiral, Lakesha, Lakesha, her cheeks round when she smiled. Orenna's molten stare. The accusation. Now at least she no longer had to see her old car on the street and turn the corner to avoid the possibility of that stare. Reading Michael Keener's story that someone had broken into the pound and been scared off. Whoever it was had been trying to get into the area where dogs are held for rabies quarantine or for biting—legal matters—and the only ones there were Artis's dogs and a chow that had nipped a mailman.

Lakesha running, with her white coat open and her book bag dragging.

Yesterday she had walked past Dave's classroom and glanced in. He was bending over the Pennell boy, lining something out, his forefinger moving slowly across the page of a book. Jim looked up, and she had turned away and walked quickly before that focus could lock on her.

Tracey lay flat, the covers kicked in a pile at her feet. The air was cool but damp and clinging; she felt heavy, unable to move.

The dog lunging into the car. Huge head and bloody saliva as it snarled. She slammed that head in the door until she could shut the door. She couldn't get out of the car. Couldn't. Couldn't.

They didn't know. The teachers who thought she was aloof. The parents who thought she was just "Northern" and that way. The man in the home center who had seen her studying the racks of PVC pipe and given her his business card, a plumber. She told him she thought she could manage this, and he looked her up and down. "I guess you're one of those in-de-pen-dent women," he drawled. "You do it all for yourself."

When she went out with her cart, Artis's red truck was pulled up behind hers, and the plumber was leaning on the mirror, guffawing over some joke. Tracey hung back a moment at the entrance, then pushed her cart into the parking lot and through the pools of light to her car. She loaded the trunk and slammed it shut. She heard the truck go into gear. That was all he wanted, just to intimidate her. But when she came back from putting the cart in its corral, the plumber was gone, but the truck was idling behind her car.

"Tracey," Artis said. He rubbed his jaw, then set both hands on the steering wheel. "I guess you heard the coroner cleared my son's dogs."

"That's not exactly right," she came back. "He said he couldn't tell."

Artis looked away but she could see his mouth working.

"Yeah, might could be. Comes down to you."

"I saw them."

"What exactly did you see? You didn't stick around long enough to do anything. You're guilty enough for leaving." He raised his hands from the steering wheel as though to slam them down, but instead set them gently back. She fixed her attention on his hands, not his face, and saw his knuckles go white. "I don't know what you think you're getting out of this, except getting back at me."

"Move your truck," she said. "I'm going home."

Tracey had watched Artis pull away, the truck swaying and squealing out into the street.

She fell back onto the hot, damp bed. Awake in the dark, staring up with eyes too hot to shed tears. As long as she kept moving she was safe, walking fast on the sidewalk past the house where the Kozlowski boys lived, where they lounged on the porch. She was afraid of their eyes.

As long as she kept moving. Tracey rolled onto her side and curled around the truth. If she stayed, all the worst things that could happen surely would. A moving target was hard to hit.

She ran away when Lakesha needed her. There wasn't any way to shade that. She'd justified it—the dogs were terrifying, she would have been injured or killed as well, and no help then for Lakesha—but she knew that nearly every one of the people who looked at her in the street and sized her up thought, *I would have done differently. I would have thrown myself onto those animals, saved the child.*

Some people hunkered down when trouble came, digging in. She had always been a rabbit, dodging what dogged her. Tracey could count the incidents, hostile girls in middle school, troublesome boys in high school, her grandmother's death, her parents' divorce. What could she remember from that time but their twisted faces, words spitting past each other? She hadn't slowed down long enough for the pain to hook her. She'd run from her own divorce, from Carl's presence in the same town, from the reminders in every corner.

Tracey got up and walked to the window. The coolness soothed her.

She loved the view from here, over the trees to the fields and beyond, the low wave of worn-down mountains. This house had stood for a century. The people who built it had lived here long before that. This was a place where people found a way to stay put.

She leaned on the sill. It didn't look so much different from Ohio; in the moonlight, the tobacco looked like fields of young corn. Almost like home.

CHAPTER NINE

Dave had smelled it as soon as he stepped into the stairwell and let the door swing shut behind him. If he could, he would have backed up and made it never happen.

Trey stood in the blank back corner under the stairs, his foot grinding the dropped joint into dust and his face turned up through the hanging smoke to see who was coming.

"Hey, Mr. Fordham," he said. "Haven't forgot your class." There was a little uplift at the end. Hope? Trey stood still, his foot planted on the evidence, his angular face showing neither anger nor fear.

"I'm sorry to see this, Trey. We'll have to go upstairs."

Trey didn't move a muscle, but his eyes hooded. "I was just standing here, y'know? This a popular corner."

"Trey. Don't try to get over on me."

"Shit, man. You take me up to Buckner and it's all over." Trey reached up and draped his hands over the metal railing. At 16 he was a man already, not powerful but tall and quick. Dave focused on his hands, the long fingers, the broad palms. He knew that when the paperwork was done on this incident, Trey would be out. A man grown and expected to find his way with eight full grades of education.

"Mr. Fordham." Dave looked up. Trey leaned back, his arms holding up his weight. "I was good in your class, I was, you know I was good. You leave this, I be clean …"

He felt the two-way radio hanging on his belt, the pressure of

Trey's attention on his face, his hands, the radio. Trey *had* been good in class, or at least non-combative, present in body but never in spirit. He saw him as he had been the other morning, sprawled on the couch, waiting for someone to decide his fate.

"It's not good enough, Trey." His jaw set at that, and Dave saw the muscle pop out in his cheek. "You can't keep sliding. You can do better for yourself."

Dave unhooked the radio. That fast, Trey shifted, was just a step away, face to face now, his breath hot and marijuana-sweet.

"Don't push me," Trey said, very low.

"Don't—make it worse." Dave turned his head away. He felt the radio shudder in his hand, realized it was his own hand shaking, and clamped down hard. He tried to focus on that and not on the fear that tore at him from the inside. Trey's body was *that* close, *that* fast, taking all the air out of the musty space at the bottom of the stairs. Dave could imagine Trey's hands moving as fast, imagined the fisted weight of them against his face, the clench of one around a knife or a brick, and the parting of his skin.

"What you doin', man?"

Dave looked at his hand, made it open and his thumb press the hot button that buzzed the school resource officer.

"What I'm required to."

"Fuck!" Trey moved and he braced himself for the blow, but Trey feinted past him and took the stairs in two bounds, his boots skidding on the metal plates as he reached the ground level and slammed outside.

"Buckner here."

Dave stared at the radio.

"Buckner here. Come in."

"Hello." *What a civilian.* "Uh, this is Dave Fordham. We have, we had, an incident on the north stairwell at the basement."

"Anyone down?"

"No," he answered, resisting the urge to say, "Negative."

"10-4. On my way."

The SRO came in his blue uniform, took an evidence baggie out of one of the woven leather pockets on his belt, gathered the joint and wrote down what Dave had to say in a black notebook. Dave stared at the door that had shut behind Trey, the window empty of his shape or shadow. There would be a report to sign later and put in Trey's file, copies for the juvenile court and the central office, a visit with Trey's aunt. He shifted from good foot to bad foot to good foot, as though he were the one being interrogated, arrested, charged.

Dave still had one class to teach and there wasn't anyone to cover for him. He stayed at the front of the classroom the entire time, lecturing, postponing the small group discussions in the lesson plan. He couldn't roam the aisles, put himself in reach of the big loose hands or the booted feet sticking out from under the desks.

The school day finally over, he headed for his apartment, but though he had his signal on to make the usual right at the light, instead he made an abrupt turn left. It wasn't the direct route to Burnt Cabin Road, and Dave wouldn't have said he was even headed for Tracey's, until after some aimless turns he realized that he was—and had to admit he needed someone to listen.

He bumped down the lane, committed then. Tracey was on the porch, sitting straight to see who was on the way. Bottles and rusty implements lined the porch railings. She got up, the metal glider squawking loud enough for him to hear over the engine, and raised her hand to show him where to park. As he pulled around, one of those wild cats skittered from its hiding place under a straggly azalea.

"Hey," he said, embarrassed now for arriving without notice, without invitation.

"Hi there." She stepped to the edge of the porch. "I just got some tea. You want some?"

He blessed her for the hospitality that did not demand what brought him out here. He found a bare place on the railing and sat down. She came back with her own glass refilled and a glass for him, tinkling with slivers of ice.

"Unsweetened?" she checked.

"That's right."

She grinned and swirled the ice in her glass. "You sure you're from around here, where you can get cavities just by looking at the sweet tea?"

"Pretty sure." Dave took a long drink, suddenly thirsty, suddenly hungry, the knot in his stomach unraveling.

"How was your day?"

"It was a day. Six students absent in one class, two new ones to replace them. Jim Pennell failed the quiz, though I can't understand why—he might get out of there if he'd make an effort." He noticed her face stiffen at the mention of the Pennells and let the subject drop. Now that he was here, still in his school clothes while she was in jeans and sweatshirt, the problem with Trey receded. Just for a while, he wanted to enjoy the conversation, without school problems. He set his emptied glass on the railing and picked up a flat bottle with a narrow neck, stained with dirt. "Old," he said.

"It's a medicine bottle, some kind of bitters. I found it down in the farm dump—I guess an archeologist would call it a midden."

He had a vision of Tracey in khaki, auburn hair streaming out from under a pith helmet, excavating an Egyptian statue from a pile of sand.

"I was wandering around right after I bought the place, looking up in the trees like a goober," she admitted, laughing, "and when I stepped the whole area just caved in under me."

Dave squinted, thinking about the slide through old garbage.

"It wasn't so bad," she said, picking up on his thoughts. "It hasn't been used since the '50s, my guess. I kicked around a little, and turned up one of these old bottles. That's when I knew it must have been the dump from way back, and I got excited. I used to do this in Ohio."

"Dumpster diving?"

"Give me a break," she said. "Come on, I'll show you."

He only considered his slick-soled shoes for a minute. "Sure."

They walked down the flagstone path, turning behind the coop to thread through the remains of the farm—machine shed, chicken coop and the tobacco-curing barn, a tall log-built structure leaning under a tangle of scuppernong vines. He saw a black-and-white cat watching them from under the grapevines. Garland, he recalled. A calico darted across the path in front of them. "Which one is that?"

"Quentina. I haven't seen her in a while—I thought she might be dead."

They followed a bit of an old farm road along a field hummocked with rough hay. He didn't think she meant to move fast but her strides were long; she seemed accustomed to covering ground. He had to work to keep up, with his foot aching in its brace and the school shoes slipping on the grass. A brisk little breeze moved the greening branches of the trees and the brown tatters of last year's grass.

She dove into a patch of woods where the ground sloped toward a little stream, and the dump straggled down that slope toward the resting place of an ancient refrigerator and two rusted wagon wheels. Tracey stopped and spread her arms like she was opening the gates to an elegant garden. And oddly enough, Dave could almost see it that way. Trilliums raised white triangles over the leaf-litter, and Virginia bluebells and other glimmering pale flowers he couldn't name seemed all the more brilliant in the dim afternoon light. Dogwood spread layers of white blossoms among the leafing branches of bigger trees. The dump site was lumpy from her digging, some of it covered with last fall's leaves and some of it freshly opened, the thin layer of loam split down into Carolina red clay.

"I've figured out where the older stuff is, over here," she said, grabbing a short-handled shovel that leaned into the crotch of a tree. Tracey went down the slope and across the tongue of debris, set the rusty blade in the ground and began to lift clods of earth, roots, stones, trash. Sifting, she let each shovelful fall to the side.

One clod caught Dave's attention, and he bent over and began to poke at it with a stick. The straight edge, with some probing, turned out to be a belt buckle. It was corroded and didn't look all that old, or that valuable.

"Look," she said, turning over a little stoneware bowl. The inside was decorated with a band of purple flowers, the design marred by rust spots.

"Pretty," he said.

"I've found some others, all broken. From the '30s, the best I can tell."

Dave felt awkward. She had become so intent he wondered if she remembered he'd come along. She moved over, dug deeper, then bent and lifted a dark blue jar into the light and smiled at him so purely happy he felt a rush of joy as well.

"Cobalt," she said, and he went over to look. It was a small bottle, the stopper missing, an intense deep blue. "If you hold it up to the light, you can see how rich the color is, almost a purple in it."

"How old is that?"

"I don't know. Maybe turn of the century." She rubbed the bottle on her shirt. It was the color of—he tried to place it. Ocean night, clear moonless sky over tropical ocean. Maybe that came close.

Tracey turned the bottle in her hand, buffed it on her shirt again like an apple she was preparing to eat. "So, how far back do we go here? How long have people been here?"

"The native population, Cashie, Saponi. Then colonial settlement, English, German coming in from the coast, then Quakers coming down the wagon road from Pennsylvania. The Revolution. You know there was a major battle to the west of us, the Battle of Guilford Courthouse. General Greene let Cornwallis chase him back and forth until his army was worn down and sick. That's why he lost at Yorktown, you know—he'd used up his troops in the Carolinas."

Tracey nodded. He imagined she knew most all this from books, as he knew it from family stories and roadside plaques studied from the back seat of the Mercury.

"Where I grew up, you'd never know the Revolution was fought south of Valley Forge," she said, and kicked lightly at some excavated earth. "So there might be things that far back?"

"Probably not. There wasn't any real farming out here 'til the early 1800s. Tobacco, corn, a little cotton."

"Slaves."

"Yes. But in a smaller way than on the coast or in the Deep South."

"I don't imagine they noticed the difference."

Dave flushed. "I imagine they did. Read up on the rice plantations, or the canal building over in the Dismal Swamp—the malaria and the snakes. This region was half settled by Quakers and Mennonites, real troublemakers, abolitionists—Jefferson Davis despaired of maintaining control here."

"Hmmm."

"It was a lot more complicated than it seems."

Tracey started digging again. He saw how her lips were compressed, holding something back, and wondered if he'd sounded like a Rebel apologist. But a stubborn streak wouldn't let him say as much. Instead, he knelt on the broken ground and began to poke through the dirt that came flying way too fast from the hole Tracey was excavating. As he started to toss aside a clump, a flash of white showed among the webby roots and he pulled back. He broke the clump apart, carefully, until he saw what it was—a carved flower, nestled among the roots like the inversions of reality that make sense in dreams.

"Hey, Tracey," he said.

She leaned on the shovel and looked at him. Her face was damp and her hair clung to her forehead.

He ran his thumb over the carved surface, smooth and almost warm. "It's ivory, I think." He bent forward and held it out to her.

"You're right, I think. Ivory." She let the shovel fall and stood straight, easing her muscles with a lean to the left and one to the right. He saw pain crunch her forehead and realized she must have a bad back.

"I could use a stretch, too." Dave stretched to pull the kinks from his own back, used a tree as a handhold to help him sit down where the slope was clear of catbrier. His feet pushed out stiffly between clusters of bluebells.

Tracey sat down, still intent on his find. She spit on her fingers and rubbed some of the crust from the flower. "It's a rose, like a wild rose I think." She turned it over and back. "Maybe from a hatpin? Or a brooch? It's not a button."

Here he was, sitting on a flowered bank, beside a beautiful country-bred lass who wasn't afraid to spit. Birds were singing, one of them with long, melodious phrases. He could hear Oberon's song: "I know a bank where the wild thyme blows/Where oxlips and the nodding violet grows." As he considered her fine straight nose and elegant lips, he thought he might as well be Bottom, wearing the mule's head well suited to his nature.

"So, how old is this farm?"

"Early 19th century. This was once all part of the Chalmers Holding."

She nodded in recognition of a name found all over the county.

"Four big plantations were made out of the original survey. This part was the Pettigrews. After the war, the plantations were broken up—Abner Pettigrew served in the Confederate government and he lost his property—but the family hung onto parts of it through purchase. The Floyds, who bought what you know as the Floyd place, were a collateral line. Cousins."

"You know a lot for an English teacher."

"Family history," he said, then regretted that—he didn't want her to think he was a snob for his Pettigrew roots. "I surely am from around here." He smiled, and she did, too. Dave felt the swell of unexpected pride—this was his place, and the yeasty smell of the opened ground was as good as bread baking in the kitchen.

"I guess you get tired of Yankees."

He shrugged. "Just the ones who come here for the weather and criticize everything else. The criticism is all right, things aren't perfect. It's just the stereotypes, the idea that things haven't changed in the South."

"It doesn't help when people see the Confederate flag flying," she said, but not as sharply as she often remarked.

He wasn't going to go there. Instead, he began to talk about how, despite the past, that blacks and whites lived and worked together a lot closer here than they did in the North. "This is how I put it—tell me how many black friends you had up North? Not people you worked with, but real friends, people whose house you visited?"

Tracey sat forward and wrapped her arms around her knees. "Where I grew up, there weren't any black people. Just white-socks farmers."

"We're all bound together. It's like the names, the black Chalmerses and white Chalmerses, the white Floyds and the black Floyds. That goes a long way back, and there's a lot of pain, but this is still our home. Our land. We all come out of the same red dirt. Blood and clay."

She looked through the trees toward the open field. "I wonder," she began, then, stopped. "I wonder what the black Chalmerses think when they look at the big houses and the pastures and fields. I mean, they built all of that, they made it, and it's beautiful and in some ways I guess I'd be proud, but it's not theirs."

Dave almost said something about white tenant farmers, but he'd had enough of a say already.

She stood and gathered up the flowered dish and the blue bottle and put the ivory carving in her pocket. "Something else I want to show you before it gets dark." And she took off.

He brushed leaves from his pants and went after her.

On the other side of the field, a wide-spreading magnolia and some cedar trees shaded a square where family burials had been made. There was no fence, the space marked more by how the deep year-round shade kept the grass thin around the gravestones.

"Floyds, Proctors, and McCustons," she said. "The oldest ones are all Floyds."

Lichen crusted the old stone, and sooty streams wept down the flat markers. Dave bent to read them.

"Lawd-a-mercy," he said, putting on his auntie voice, "you named your cats for the dead!"

"That's a bad thing?" She had that tone, half smart-aleck, half worried she'd offended.

Dave grinned. "They probably like hearing their names."

A marble stone gleamed whiter than the rest—Mary McCuston Floyd, beloved mother, born June 14, 1852, gone to her reward Dec. 2, 1912. "A good woman is worth more than rubies." It looked like it had been cleaned, and Tracey admitted she had tried, but stopped when she found it disconcertingly bright among the gray others.

One marker was inscribed CSA, with a death date of 1863, but no name but Proctor. The latest burial was in 1935, a granite stone for Celia Floyd, who died an old woman. Tracey bent and pulled creeping-charlie away from the base of Celia's stone.

"People used to keep the burying-grounds clean," Dave said, remembering with a sudden pang his grandfather's hand shears, the sound of them as he clipped around the stones. He'd spent the time looking for fence lizards while the old people worked, the smell of cut grass and weeds sharp around them. That was the smell, the sap of the creeper pulled and chopped away.

"I guess there's no one around anymore," Tracey said.

"Did they do that in Ohio? Dinner on the ground and mowing?"

"Memorial Day, I guess." She was wandering away, toward the

dimmest corner, the shadows pulling together where the trees met. "Putting out flags and plastic flowers. But most of the places are perpetual care so it doesn't matter much." She stopped talking, stopped where she was, staring down at a statue. Dave followed her and saw a lamb, the curls on its back smoothed by the weather but the letters of "Enoch Floyd" clear where they were inscribed on a scroll below its folded legs. The grave was short. A child's grave.

Dave thought it was an awfully small space. He wondered if she was considering Lakesha. Dying young. A chill went across him—the chill of someone walking across your grave. He'd never considered his mortality until three years ago. He'd not considered much else until pretty recently. Dave wrapped his arms close around himself. It was cold in the shadows, under these trees where the winter seemed to have hung on past its time.

"Cold?" Her voice was gentle.

He nodded, moved into a patch of sun and let the golden light pour into him. Something shuddered loose deep inside, like ice cracking free from a shore.

"I had a confrontation at school today," he said.

Tracey was standing beside him now, facing the same red sunset. Her hair caught fire in that light, the thin breeze lifting a few hairs like sparks, and Dave had to close his eyes to continue.

"Trey was smoking a joint in the north stairwell. Don't know if he didn't hear me coming, or just didn't care. I turned him in. I was that close to not doing it, but the word would have got around and I couldn't have controlled a class then." His stomach clenched. "And it wouldn't have done Trey any good either."

Tracey gave a clipped laugh. "I don't imagine he saw it that way."

"Yeah, well, he's been slipping under the radar for so long maybe he needs to deal with these things." Stung, Dave answered with a kind of toughness and assurance that he didn't feel at all.

"What happened?"

"He ran off. I thought he was going to hit me, for a minute. He came right up in my face, but then he took off." The memory made him flinch, and he hoped she hadn't seen it.

"I hate to say it, but it was inevitable. He wasn't getting anywhere at school, you know that. He was just biding his time—I'll bet he's on a bus to Atlanta right now. Don't blame yourself."

"I don't."

"You didn't push him out."

"That's not what I'm afraid of," Dave muttered.

There was a long pause. He felt the ice grinding in that wintry river, clogged, the sounds like a rock quarry as the blocks worked against each other. Then suddenly it was all fluid, moving, the ice splitting apart and sailing for open water.

"They used to call me 'Bama. Up north," he began. "I was right out of grad school, full of all the best pedagogical techniques that Carolina could stuff me with. I was going to save the world." He saw Tracey put a closed fist inside her other hand, holding them safely together the way someone does when they are afraid of being asked a difficult question. "I got the first job I applied for, Baltimore City. I found an apartment about a mile from the school, and at orientation I learned about school resource officers and metal detectors and gang signs and colors."

"Must have been culture shock," she offered.

"Yeah boy. Raleigh was about the biggest place I'd spent any time, and you've seen Raleigh."

She nodded, and he wondered if he should go on. If self-pity would show through, if she would be revolted by his cowardice.

"And then?"

"I'd never seen kids like that. The good ones were running scared all the time, didn't show up for class because they couldn't get past the gunfire in the projects, while the bad ones hung in the halls and sold crack until they got kicked out, and then they kept on selling by passing it through the chain-link fence."

"But you stayed."

Dave saw the red-brick face of the high school, walling in the students, walling out the parents, the community, any hope. Black iron bars on the tall windows dated from its construction, but looked like they had been meant all along for this time, this violent siege.

"There was one." She glanced at him, and he could have said what she was thinking. The teacher's apologia—if I can reach just one, then I'll be doing my job. Just one. "Anthony. Anthony Tarleton.

He was a genius, I think, brilliant. But his eyes were flat, he kept them flat, so that no one could tell he cared. I never raised a spark in them, as much as I tried."

Now the words came in a rush and he stumbled with the urgency of confession.

"I was walking home. It was winter—dark already, slush on the ground, more coming. Not far—it was not very far from the school. I turned the corner and came on a group." He thought about turning corners, turning into the stairwell, turning down that street instead of going one more block. "Five or six of them. Kids. Men. They watched me and I kept walking, trying not to look at them. They blocked the sidewalk and I stepped out into the street. I remember the cold water going into my shoes."

As the sun dipped below the trees and the light went gray, Dave felt his stomach clench. No air to speak, barely to breathe, the grim night closing cold hands around his heart. He pulled his arms tighter around the core of his body.

Stop it, he told himself. Stop living there.

He breathed deeply until the fear passed, and then he told the rest.

"One of them pushed me down. Then they started. The first foot caught me in the stomach and made me roll up. I covered my head. I knew they were going to kill me. They hit—once I wished they'd shoot me and get it over with. I rolled into the water and started to choke, crawled out of it, and I looked up and I swear I saw Anthony."

"Oh God," Tracey breathed.

"I don't know. I thought it was him then, but lately I don't know. The dark, the hoods and baggy pants. The cops never arrested anyone. They said I walked into a deal or a gang meeting. Case closed." His heart still lurched at the vision of Anthony, and he thought that during the beating he had called out to him.

"How badly were you hurt?"

"I laid there for a long time, until an off-duty cab driver saw me. He thought I was dead. He shouldn't have gotten out of his car to check, not in that neighborhood, but he did—he stopped and looked at me. I'll never forget his voice. He was from deep in the South, and it sounded so wonderful. 'You dead?' he asked. 'I'm hurt,' I told him. 'You shot?' 'I'm hurt.'" He relaxed a little, remembering the man's rich, deep voice, for all the world like Old Man River. "Then he went to his cab and I thought surely he would drive away, but he called dispatch and came back with a blanket. 'I keeps it for pregnant ladies, should they take a notion to let the chile fly on the way to the hospital.'"

Dave stopped. Still the question was unanswered. "The police came first, and they tried to talk to me. I guess I wasn't making sense, but it seemed more like they were interrogating me. Then the paramedics got there and started with the needles. When I woke up, the doctor told me the damage: ruptured spleen, four broken ribs, broken ulna, facial cuts and contusions, a concussion. And the foot." How to tell that? "The foot was still with me, as they say, and me with the foot. That—that's when I had wanted them to shoot me. When that happened. I didn't know what caused that kind of pain, until the police told me—an iron pipe, they beat on my foot with an iron pipe. Smashed the bones, severed the nerve. Inflammation, bone chips, tissue breakdown. When the doctors told me I'd wear a brace for the rest of my life, they reminded me I was lucky to have a foot to wear it on."

She put her hand on his arm, lightly, right above where his hand clutched his elbow to keep the warmth in. He smiled at her—she was almost of a height so he didn't have to look down but straight into her eyes, which were wide and somber. Mourner's eyes. He felt his smile slip away and turned away to hide what was moving in his heart. The light was purple, fading. Soon it would be dark enough not to worry what his face showed.

"When I got out of the hospital, I gave my key to the super and had my things packed and shipped home. I went to Durham for therapy. I learned to wear the brace and walk again. A little differently."

"You do well, considering."

"And then I came home. Really home, to Momma." He unfolded his arms, let them drop, her hand sliding off and the cold air hitting his chest. Crawling home, he thought, and the line from Robert Frost came up like bile, the way it always did, "Home is the place where, when you have to go there, they have to take you in."

As though she heard it too, she answered. "Sometimes you

think you can get free by leaving home. Sometimes all you do is get another angle on what you want, or can't have. Sometimes you have to go back."

"It was perfect, the final irony. The only job I could find was at the alternative school," he said, talking to keep the air moving between them. "All those oversized, angry, messed-up kids. Men. Tracey, I'm scared every day. Not just of them, though I am scared of them. I'm afraid I've turned into a racist as well as a coward." He heard the small noise she made, reassuring, and he would have none of it. "The black kids just send a shudder through me—the shitkicker boots, the way they wear those oversized clothes, and I keep looking for a gun or an iron pipe to come out. I can't help it. I can't even look them in the eyes."

"You're not a coward, and you're not a racist." Tracey didn't try to move him, but she moved herself, facing him, making him look at her. "You're like a man who's been in battle."

Her voice lay on him like the warmth of her hand, and he wanted that reassurance again so badly. "I remember the cab driver. He was black. And I try to balance that, how he stopped for me, and talked with me and covered me up. A good man, a brave one. But I'm still afraid." Now that he had said it, Dave was horrified at himself, at this revelation, but at the same time he felt blown clear, hollow.

"You're not the only one who's afraid," she said, and he caught the bitterness in her tone, a familiar sound.

"The dogs?"

She nodded. "And other times. I'm a coward, if you want to be plain about it."

"I don't think that's so."

And he felt buoyed by giving her his words, his compassion, as she had first. The oppression lifted from his heart. Not a soul down here knew all what had happened. Not an old school friend, or a cousin or an uncle. His mother had known, but she was gone. He felt strange for that, to be so disconnected—but now, maybe, Tracey—he pushed that away, a wild wing of hope and desire he couldn't catch. Another line of poetry came quickly, the answer that home was "something you somehow haven't to deserve."

"Coming back here. Coming home. I made so little of my life after such big plans," he said.

"Plans are fine." She held the little dish in her hands, turning it over and back. "The people who threw this away had plans. Whatever they were. We just keep putting one foot in front of the other."

"In the dark."

"In the dark, sometimes." Then he saw the flash of her smile. "And we'll be caught in the dark if we don't get a move on."

Their eyes had adapted, apparently, because the path was easy going back to the house. The breeze had died down and it seemed warmer.

The house showed big and white and almost familiar. Dave was headed for the front door when Tracey turned toward the side porch and the hand pump. "The drains are bad enough—I try not to clog them up," she said. "This is where the summer kitchen used to be."

He worked the pump handle until, with a grinding sound and the smell of loosened rust, water gurgled up and gushed from the spout. Tracey squatted to one side and held the ivory piece under the stream, picked at the dirt deep in the crevices. The water splashed in time to his working, the uneven ploop of water on slate and the creak of the handle the only sounds. She set the ornament aside and started on the flowered bowl. Even in the dim light he could see the pattern emerging, caked grime yielding to plain water. Her hands were cold against his as the dish passed between them, and he felt a rush of desire as her fingers slipped away.

He turned the dish over, concentrating on the wreath of roses inside the rim. He would not reveal the want that ached in him.

"Hey, how about some water, fella?"

He set the bowl on the grass and put his weight against the arthritic pump handle a couple more times. The water resumed. Tracey shook the bottle and poured it out, ran it full again and shook and poured.

"That's the worst of it," she said. "My hands are frozen—let's get inside."

At the door, she reached inside and the kitchen flooded with light. He followed her, tentative—he'd only been there a couple of times, and never inside the house, where the kitchen held the day's warmth and the furnishings looked like they'd been there forever. He sat at the enamel table with a leaf that drew out, just like his grandmother Weaver's, and watched her move around, fixing coffee and trying to conceal the mess she'd left from the morning.

"Can you drink it black?"

"Sure," he said, though he never did.

She hummed something as she worked. He studied the old pictures, the worn canisters, a calendar from the year he was born. He wondered if they were hers, her family's, or the history some folks make from flea markets. He saw how she'd arranged the bottles on the windows where the light would pour through them. And then she turned from the sink and looked straight at him, and he wondered if she could tell he had stopped breathing.

CHAPTER TEN

In the Saul County Courthouse, people waited for the law in the echoing corridors of the second floor, some crammed tightly together on the straight oak benches, others scattered singly along the walls. Tracey wondered what they were here for, indictments or family court or drug cases, and imagined they glanced at her with the same concealed interest. The district attorney's office had asked her to make a statement—a deposition for the case before the grand jury. Two earlier appointments had been cancelled. Each time she'd barely slept the night before, the facts of Lakesha's death blurring into the edges of horrifying dreams. Today, again, she was jittery with coffee, her nerves taut but her mind sluggish with lack of sleep.

She wandered back and forth, looking at the tax sale notices curling on their bulletin board, looking at the courthouse regulations. The first floor of the building, where she paid her taxes, smelled like the street—diesel exhaust and dust and a faint odor of stale urine. But this floor smelled like the disused stacks of art books and military manuals at the state college she'd attended. Musty. Mildewy. As though the slow pace of justice allowed everything to be furred with slow rot. The walls were painted mustard yellow and the marble underfoot carried that tone, also the light fixtures hanging from the high ceiling. Even what was natural was stained, the dirty illumination through the bird-limed glass dome, the thin morning that made its way from the east windows across the court clerk's office and out through the frosted glass doors.

She was called away from consideration of a mural of seated justice by the secretary, who leaned out from the double doors and beckoned.

The assistant district attorney was a little man, the walnut shade of his skin making him seem even smaller, more contained in the tight jacket of his brown suit, the sleeves pulled back as though they were too short, revealing white cuffs and thin brown wrists and a heavy gold watch. His name was Ervin Dupree and he had the mild look of a Unitarian minister.

He rested his hands flat on the table between them. *Laying my hand on the table*. Was that part of his performance as a prosecutor?

"Miss Gaines," he began, and she shivered. It sounded too much like the prelude to a damaging question, an interrogation. "Your deposition will assist this office in presenting the matter of Lakesha Sipe to the grand jury for possible indictment of Artis Pennell on manslaughter charges."

Tracey flinched. "Manslaughter?"

"This office made the decision to bring the case to the grand jury for deliberation because the law is far from clear in this matter. The county's leash law, as it currently exists, applies only to incorporated towns and designated areas of public recreation. Still, we believe the law makes the owner responsible for the actions of his animals as he would be for any personal property—for instance, should he leave his car in gear and it strike an innocent bystander."

"Is there jail time?"

He blinked and looked at her as though she had interrupted his opening argument. "Prison time is an included penalty, though the sentence may be reduced or suspended."

Tracey wasn't sure she wanted to put anyone behind bars. Artis should have kept his dogs home, should have told the truth—but Jim, what about him, without mother or father? Dupree's eyes seemed to refocus behind his wire-rimmed glasses, the mildness gone. "The girl's death demands an accounting. Justice is, as they say," and he passed his hands across his eyes but did not close them. "But forgiveness is a matter between the soul and God, and not a concern of the law."

Tracey felt herself understood and in some way dismissed. She had underestimated Ervin Dupree.

The secretary came in with a notepad and sat down behind a tape recorder. She nodded and started the machine.

It wasn't so difficult at first. Dupree asked the basic questions, who she was, where she lived and worked. Tracey recalled lunch duty and bus duty, and then her drive home.

"You were following a bus?" he asked.

"Bus No. 41. I catch up to it on Burnt Cabin Road, most days, and follow it until I turn off at my lane."

"Off Burnt Cabin Road."

"Yes."

"Does it make a stop at Downey Trailer Homes Park No. 1 before you turn off to your house?"

She nodded, and he raised his hand, palm up, as though preparing to support the weight of her words.

"Yes. It stops at Downey's trailer park."

"Did it stop that day?"

"Yes."

"How many students got off the bus at that stop?"

"Just Lakesha—Lakesha Sipe. She's the only school student living there right now."

"How do you know Lakesha Sipe? Is she one of your students?"

"No—I see her on bus duty. I see her when she gets off the bus. She's just a little girl—once I bought her a coat because I thought she looked cold out there."

Dupree inclined his head, just the smallest bit.

"And what did you see when she got off the bus that evening?"

"The dogs," she said, realized she had whispered, and started again. "The dogs. I had seen them running across the field. Then I saw them headed for the trailer park road."

"How many?" he prompted.

"Four. I didn't think that could happen—what happened. I thought they might scare her. I called to her, to Lakesha, about the dogs." Tracey tried to recall exactly what had happened, exactly what she had said to the deputy that night, but the edges blurred the way memories always did for her. The dogs were real, running hard across

the raw plowed field. And Lakesha in her white coat. Pressure built
in her chest, her throat. She stared at the Roman numerals on the
door window, each standing on its serif, cool as justice, distant as
marble columns.

"And then."

The whole thing flooded back. "Lakesha began to run. The dogs
went after her. I honked and drove down the road, trying to distract
them or scare them off. The dogs—two big ones, the Rottweiler and
the boxer, and the other two."

"Was Lakesha screaming?"

She couldn't remember. Maybe. She remembered the sound of the
dogs snarling when she opened the door. But no memory of Lakesha's
voice. She must have blocked it out, surely she had screamed.

"I don't remember."

Her hands were shaking, and Tracey clutched them together
under the table. She wished Dave were waiting outside for her. She
would have peace of mind if he were out there sitting on a bench,
head tilted a little sideways like he did when he was thinking, but
he was at school. She hadn't asked him to come.

She felt the assistant district attorney and the secretary waiting,
felt the weight of the legal system descending on her, and she stilled
her hands and went on.

"The dogs knocked her down. I couldn't see Lakesha, she was on
the ground, and I was afraid to drive any closer. I honked the horn
and yelled but the dogs didn't leave. I opened the door ... the car
door ... the dog tried to get to me and I slammed the door on its
head. Over and over. Finally it gave up. There wasn't anyone around."

"You didn't see anyone in the trailers, or on the road?"

"No one."

"You didn't get out?"

Tracey looked down at her knotted hands. "The dogs wouldn't
let me," she said, and couldn't bring herself to add, I was afraid. She
burned at her cowardice, how deeply it ate into her soul, how far back
it went. Fearful nights after Carl left. Her grandmother shriveling
day by day. A moving herd of cows, massive and mindless. *The dark.*
Blindfolded by older children who slipped away from the game. She
called, turning in panic until she ran into a thorny bush and yanked

off the blindfold. When she caught up with the others dancing ahead, she was crying and bleeding. Her grandmother, fallen and bleeding in the dark she'd tried to make gentle for a frightened child.

"Continue, please," he said softly, calling her back. She focused on the white cuffs between his wrists and coat sleeves, pure and clerical.

"I backed up and went home to call for help. It was the closest I could. I called 911 and I went back." Guilt lashed her, thinking that a phone call was enough, that a white coat could protect. A chill shook her, the memory of the dark road and the cold wind, the odor of stale ditch-water and the metallic whiff of blood. "I found Lakesha down in the water, in the ditch. I covered her up and held her until the ambulance got there."

"The dogs were gone at that point."

"Yes."

"And you identified those dogs to Sergeant Findley?"

The tape recorder whirred. "There were four dogs. Two of them I didn't know, a collie-type and something else, short-legged, but with a big head like a mastiff. The other two I recognized, a black Rottweiler and a boxer mix, black and brown color."

"How did you recognize them?"

"I saw them in Artis Pennell's truck, several times."

"How do you know Artis Pennell?"

"He's a neighbor—his property abuts mine. We have seen each other in town, at the post office." She pressed her lips tight, fearing they would tremble or let her say what she shouldn't. "And I have taught his son Jim."

"How do you know his dogs?"

"The black one wears a red collar. That's easy to spot," she said. "They were his dogs. I've seen them several times."

Dupree opened a folder and took out some glossy photos. He spread them in front of her. A Rottweiler, a brindled dog, their faces emerging from the dark concrete kennel and crossed by chain-link fence. Their eyes were red from the flash.

"Are these the dogs?"

She stared at the red eyes, the dog faces that were not excited or aggressive or frightened, just confused. "They look like them. Yes.

The red collar. And the brindled one is unusual looking. Yes, these are the dogs."

Dupree seemed satisfied. She was surprised herself at how well she had ended, after the shaky start. There wasn't any doubt those were the Pennell dogs. The plain truth. But as she half listened to details of the grand jury proceedings and the expected trial date, Tracey wondered if telling the truth had been the best thing after all.

Leaving the office, she looked toward the bench where she'd visualized Dave waiting. An old woman was sitting there in a flowered dress, very erect with her black pocketbook upright in her lap. The woman saw that she was staring and stood up as though expecting something. Tracey hurried away.

The doors opened on the courtroom and people spilled out. If there were losers in that case, they went out a back entrance, because all these people seemed very pleased. The men slapped each other on the back and women laughed. Even a couple of children ran around as though at a picnic. Tracey glimpsed the judge in his black robes descending from the bench, and two lawyers in blue suits gathering papers at a long table. Mike Keener was among the stragglers, flipping through his spiral notebook as he walked.

Tracey wavered—should she make a point of saying hello?—but just then he looked up and smiled. "Hey!" he said.

"Hi."

"It's nice to see you again." He looked around the area as though trying to place where she'd been, or if she was with someone. She felt gratified that he seemed so pleased to run into her. He swiped his hair off his face and stuck his notebook in the pocket of his navy blazer. One corner had come unstitched.

Laughter started on one side of the crowd in the hallway and rippled across it, moving with the happy people toward the staircase down to the street. "What are they all so happy about?"

He laughed. "It's a strange case. One of those things that happens in the country. It's lunch time and I'm starved—can I tell you about it over a burger?"

It was well after 12 and she was indeed hungry. It was a surprise, her mind back somewhere in the cold dark, her stomach grumbling to the school's lockstep schedule even though her days were askew. She followed Mike's lead across the street to BeeGee's Bar-B-Que.

"So, what brought you to the halls of justice?" he asked over the top of the menu.

She guessed it was okay to say, a deposition.

"How was that?"

She shrugged. "What was going on with that case this morning?"

Mike nodded; the deflection must have been evident. "It was one of those oddball things, a family fighting over a boundary. You know those old deeds, so many paces to a gum tree, things like that, the gum tree rotted into the ground a hundred years ago. The one sure marker was the creek, but the old man said it used to run in a different bed, well over into the property that his brother had willed to his kids. I don't think the old man would have contested it, but he had kids of his own, and they pushed him until it ended up in the courts."

The food arrived and Tracey watched as Mike spread a heavy layer of salt and ketchup on his fries.

"Remember the big rain a couple of weeks ago?" He took a healthy bite out of the chopped sandwich, a soft concoction of minced-up pork, coleslaw, and red barbecue sauce. She nodded. "Toad strangler" was what Ray Koch had called it in the lounge that day. Rain so heavy it clotted the sky and drowned the fields, running floodwater over the roads in red sheets and inundating every basement in Willow Grove.

"Well, it changed the course of the stream. Broke through into the swale where the old man said it used to run. So the boundary has effectively moved, and the whole matter's moot anyway since that ground's scarcely worth the fighting over. I heard one old lady say it was providential, and maybe it was," he said.

He went after his sandwich again, was finished by the time she'd worked through half her salad.

"Sorry," said. "There's never enough time to eat. I have three stories to write this afternoon and God knows what else will happen in the meantime."

"It's the same when you teach," she said.

"Especially working like you do, at the alternative school, I'd think."

"It's a challenge." Tracey saw how the dressing had pooled with cold water in the bottom of the bowl. She pushed the salad away, done.

"You're not from around here, as they say," he said, shifting gears. "I'm from PA myself."

"Ohio."

"Lots of Rust Belt refugees around here. I didn't have any trouble tracking you down—the locals all knew about that teacher from up North who bought the old Floyd place."

She knew how inappropriate it looked—a woman teacher, single, taking on that enormous house. She rattled around in it like a pea in a can, as her grandmother used to say about her own widowhood in the home place. "It reminds me of my grandparents' home," she said. "And I like remodeling and fixing up."

"That's great," he said. "Coming home to your own place. I live in rooms with nothing but off-white walls. I bet you don't have an off-white room in the place."

She shifted in her seat, feeling like he'd sneaked a peek inside her house. "Have you moved around a lot?"

He laughed. "I started out to be a teacher, until I did my student teaching. Discovered I hated the little buggers. So I got a job at the local newspaper, and so on. One too many days the snow blew down my neck and I decided to cut what ties I had and head south. The *Citizen* isn't all that much, as papers go, but I like the area and they promised me a shot at editor after a year."

As he polished off the last of the French fries, Tracey considered his thick, coarse hair. He looked younger than he was, his leanness helping. Thirty, maybe? Mike licked the traces of ketchup from his fingers, grinned like a kid. Tracey felt a stir of interest. She pushed it down, feeling guilty yet at the same time warmed by an interior smile. She remembered Dave. He'd clutched her hands there at the pump, shaking with cold and with the effort of the walk—she'd had a pang at the pace she set, so used to her own company. And then, in the house, the conversation that went far deeper than the hug and the brushed kiss that lingered and was becoming interesting just when he pulled away. She'd been surprised to see him swing into the driveway as though accustomed to call, surprised at the confession of his damaged life, surprised then at how awkward the space became between them, as though between a couple of their students at a dance. And surprised at herself, at the desire she kept feeling for a man so like herself that she could trace the path of his thoughts, the avoidance of risk and of pain.

"Well, I gotta go."

She was startled to see Mike pushing back from the table, a five tossed by his plate for the sandwich and tip. She dug in her pocketbook and found enough singles to cover her tab. They walked out together. Mike lifted his hand and headed up the sidewalk to the paper.

Tracey found herself standing alone in the middle of the hot afternoon sidewalk, people parting around her as they went in their couples and groups. She stared at Mike's back as he half-trotted toward the storefront *Citizen* office, the notebook out of his pocket and his head bent to consider it. She wondered if he considered their lunch as an opportunity with a source, or just killing time. Worse yet if he had any inkling that this older woman might have found him interesting.

The day was squandered. She considered heading down to Raleigh, a visit to the art museum or a bookstore, but neither one enticed her. She could go home and peel back one of the panels of wainscoting in the parlor, see what was causing the dust that perpetually sifted out onto the floor. As always, there were papers to grade and lesson plans to prepare.

She wandered down the street instead, away from her car. The farmers market was set up in the square. It was still early in the garden year and the few tables showed a repetitive array of greens and onions and peas. One woman baked bread, another had pies. Jellies and jams and honey. The shadow of the Confederate monument fell over the egg man's table, making his trays of brown eggs look dusky and exotic against the washed-out brightness of the day. After the war, monument salesmen had taken to the roads, selling towns a standard Johnny Reb or Union soldier on a plinth—this looked like one of those, the face blank and the body stiff, facing north with rifle at the ready. The names of the gallant dead were familiar.

"Afternoon," said the egg man, smiling past tobacco-stained teeth.

She nodded, moved along. The doily-maker seemed to be asleep above her moving needle.

Tracey didn't stop. The market seemed forlorn, with so many empty spaces. The presence of the missing. Had they moved the chairs in Lakesha's class, to cover that space? Was there a cubby or a coathook with her name still on it, or had it been peeled away? Those who remained, the living, the abandoned, huddled in the shadow of those who were lost. Why did she keep trying to make something new on the burying-ground of the old? Carl's name still made her pupils widen as she spoke it, leaning close to the bathroom mirror as she had in college, looking to see if her eyes betrayed love. She doubted she'd ever lose that affection. Dave offered a warm companionability. And now, so easily was she drawn, she'd started to work up some kind of interest in Mike Keener. Damn fool, to be looking around for a man when she didn't know if the hurt inside her could ever be healed. And in this small town, where everyone was too close, where the options were too limited.

"Got it worked out?"

Tracey looked up. The young woman behind the checkered tablecloth was freckled, her straight blond hair cut square. She looked like a local farm girl, but her accent was pure Jersey.

"Pardon?"

"You looked like you were working something out while you were walking, came to a stop right here when you got it solved." The woman moved a jar of honey forward to fill the space. Goldhill Apiaries, a sign with fat bees and flowers. "You're that teacher, aren't you?"

Tracey stared at her. The woman looked straight back.

"Yes."

"Thought so. You get to know pretty much everybody around here. At first we transplants stick out, and then we start to blend in."

"I still stick out."

"I do once I open my mouth."

Tracey laughed. "How'd you get from New Jersey to Shawton, North Carolina?"

"A man and a plan. A man who was going to college in Chapel

Hill, and a plan to go back to the land and live the simple life. He's living in Seattle and I'm living the simple life, so I got it half right."

Tracey stuck out her hand. "Tracey."

"Gloria."

"How long you been here?"

"Six years."

Tracey wondered how that felt. She thought of the house resurrected board by board, the scraping and painting that would settle her in that place, make her part of its history. Looking at Gloria, she felt it was possible.

She bought a plastic bear filled with poplar honey, "the prettiest tasting honey you'll get on the flatlands," and took one of the cards. Gloria Ericsson. Her place was in the southeastern end of the county. Tracey promised to visit sometime, to see the bees at work.

She walked back to her car with the sun like a hand on her hair. She ducked under the flags arrayed in front of the hardware store, and when she looked up it was to see Artis standing across the street.

Tracey almost lifted her hand. He returned her gaze but there was no welcome there. Artis turned and walked down the street toward the market.

Forgiveness is a matter between the soul and God, Dupree had said.

When she got to her car, in the lot above the courthouse, she found the red pickup was parked in the next space.

CHAPTER ELEVEN

She drove down the narrow cut-across from Route 721 to Burnt Cabin, a dirt road left behind in the general improvements. Tracey took it sometimes for the joy of watching dust boil up behind her car. That morning she'd gone to Shawton and helped Dave paint the walls of his kitchen, a cheerful yellow over the dull green. They'd laughed over spilled paint and bad puns. She felt good if a little raw from scrubbing off the spatter, sore in the shoulders and calves. Energized.

A brown Chevy truck with a Mexican flag in the camper window was parked on the outside of the curve, its rear end cocked sideways. Tracey slowed. By the time she saw the red truck parked just beyond, it was too late to turn around. The men were facing away from the road, thank God, Artis and two Latino laborers bending and cutting flowers from the tops of tobacco plants.

She was just even with the camper when Artis turned. She was watching him more than the road and had to yank the car away from the muddy ditch on the side next to the field.

Smile, damn you.

As though he'd heard, and refused, Artis scowled and kicked at a rock in the row. It flew over the ditch and thumped onto her fender.

Tracey shoved the shifter into park and turned off the car, leaving the door open and the car blocking the road. She found where the rock had hit, spit on her fingers and rubbed at it. Under the dust the paint was marked. The chime insisted she shut the door, take her keys.

"What do you think you're doing?" She leaped across the water in the ditch—did nothing *ever* drain here?—and her paint-spotted shoes sank as she walked across the tilled ground. Artis hung his head and his mouth tightened in chagrin. She heard him say something to the men in soft Spanish. They trudged away, up the field, and Artis pulled off his cap and wiped his arm across his brow.

"I didn't mean that."

"That was a hell of a kick to not mean it. I just got the other side repainted."

Artis held his hands out, palms up. "Sorry. I'm really sorry. I don't know why I did that, really."

Tracey snorted.

"What am I supposed to say?" Frustration prickled in his voice.

"You could say you'll pay to have it fixed."

He looked over her shoulder and she glanced back to see Jim coming from the pickup, cradling an aluminum jug. Water darkened the front of his shirt

"Hi, Jim," she said, controlling her voice.

"Hey."

Jim went to his father and waited as Artis tipped back the jug and took a long drink. He stood just behind his father, backing him up. She realized how his face was beginning to hone down, becoming sharp where it had been soft and childish.

Artis unrolled a box of Winstons from his shirtsleeve. "Nice of Miz Gaines to stop and say hello to us, isn't it?"

She bit her lip. The boy didn't need to get into this. "You're helping in the field?" she asked him.

He bent his head.

"Saturday, I don't believe he's truant." Artis tossed the match and blew out a long whistle of smoke.

"I didn't mean …"

"Yet. Come auction time, it might be he'll have a flu bug."

Tracey tried to remember if he had smoked before. *Standing in the sun outside the post office. The dogs panting in the truck.* She smiled gamely, to show she wasn't baffled by how his tone shifted back and forth from contrition to mockery to gaiety. "I understand that happens when the tobacco's ready. It was deer season that emptied the schools where I came from."

"Ohio."

"Yes."

"Bit different—up there."

Tracey barely heard. He'd mentioned Ohio, remembered, made that gesture. She kept going. "Things are different, yes."

He looked closely at her, his eyes squinted against the sun. He motioned Jim to follow the laborers up the field, take them water.

"I'm sorry that misunderstandings have come between us, when we should be neighbors." There, it was out, and she heard the echo in her words. Neighbors, his voice slapping at her, *Let's just be neighbors.*

Artis stood with one arm across his chest, the other set against it and the cigarette smoldering at chin level. "So—I'll say I'm sorry for the rock. And I am. You have anything to say to me?"

From his stance, she realized too late that he wasn't offering peace—he was expecting surrender.

"Artis." She swallowed and breathed deep, in and out and in. "It's not about you and—or me."

He looked away, across the field. She saw a muscle jump in his forearm.

"I have to tell what I saw. Lakesha deserves that."

"What makes you so damned sure of yourself?"

Tracey wasn't sure she heard what she heard. Sure of herself? She doubted everything, doubted whether she'd locked the door each morning or turned off the coffee pot. She couldn't tell him how unsure she was—about everything but that night and those dogs. Those dogs she knew.

"I have to tell what happened."

"Well, you go on then and do what you gotta do. So far as the rock, send me the bill. You might try Gregory's Body Shop—they'll do a better job and charge you half what the dealership did."

"Thanks. I will."

He picked up a handful of red dirt and rubbed it between his palms; it clung to his skin, sticking to the sap from the broken flowers.

"I didn't know you had land over here," she said, trying to ease her way out.

"McGraw owns this—his widow does now," he said at last. "I'm not the quota holder." She had learned about quota, federal permission to plant, but there wasn't anything useful she could say. An urge to turn and run tightened her shoulders and clenched in her thighs. "Two acres here," he said, tossing the dirt into the field. "Used to bring in three thousand dollars. Who knows, this year."

Tracey looked at the small field, the heavy plumed leaves like in the Colonial drawings of Indians carrying tobacco that she had studied in history books. Just such red Indians and lush tobacco leaves on the Saul County flag. "It looks like a good stand," she said, then added, "good crop." The praise for Ohio corn didn't fit here, the words didn't match with the thick leaves and the blossom smell and the sharp raw sap scent that blew toward her.

"A patch of tobacco put a lot of kids through Carolina—me, for one—but I figure Jim won't have that help. If he gets that far."

"He's doing well," she offered.

"Yeah? I didn't think he had you this semester."

"I hear from the other teachers."

"That gimp?"

"If you mean Dave Fordham, yes." She wanted to say more, to wipe out that slight, but didn't.

Artis was watching Jim as he held the jug up to one of the men. Something about the way he stood, feet planted, arms akimbo and his face turned to follow the path of his son—Tracey thought he looked so much the image of this land. His sunburned arms and, yes, the soft of his stomach, a poster from the Depression or a photograph. Grown out of this soil. She almost reached toward him, impulsively needing him to accept her presence, accept her. In some way he held a key to her becoming a part of this place—the native son returned, knit into the community as though he'd never left. She was the newcomer who always seemed to be standing in the diner door, searching among the tables for a face to greet hers. If Artis gestured her inside, the smiles would be genuine and the offers heartfelt. And in the same imagining she could see Dave, sitting by himself, bent over his loneliness, an outsider in his own home place.

Artis snapped the top from a plant and rolled it between his hands. The flowers whirled back and forth, a blur of lavender and green.

"It seems a shame to have to pull them off, they look so pretty."

"Have to concentrate the energy in the leaves." Nicotiana, she connected all at once. Purple and lime-colored garden flowers, nodding on tall stalks, nothing more than fine-boned tobacco. Artis tossed the stem down. "But I don't figure you care too much about how to grow tobacco." His blue eyes were sharp.

Tracey saw the field wiggle once all over, shaken as though the world had jumped its track, the plants trembling in the sun. It was the heat, maybe, or gasoline fumes leaking from the car, the tarry scent from the snapped stems. It can make you sick, Dave said. The laborers bent and cut and tossed, the blossoms flying from their hands and settling between the crowned rows.

Artis took two steps and caught her around the waist and pulled her against him. Tracey was stunned by his body pressed against hers. Sweat came hot through her cotton blouse and then cold the instant she pushed him away. She saw that mocking smile. He bent his head, forcing a hard kiss and the taste of smoke against her lips.

Tracey pushed out with her elbows and twisted, but it wasn't until he chose to release her that she staggered back, then she was falling, tobacco plants breaking like small bones.

Sun glared in her eyes and he stood over her. Tracey had a momentary sense of some old Western, the bad guy outlined against the sky, hands on his hips, on his weapons—but Artis just put out a hand and pulled her up. She shook herself free and backed away, feeling her heart pump.

"That what you were hanging around for?"

"What the hell!" Dirt clung to the backs of her legs and she slapped it away.

"Damned if you liked it and damned if you didn't," he observed. "Women want it both ways. And neither."

"All I wanted," she said, "was to be civil. To make things better."

"Then drop it." There was no lightness in his tone, no more mockery. "You don't know my dogs from a Holstein heifer. All you're doing is costing Jim his sleep, and me, and the county money."

"It's not how you think."

Artis laughed and that made her angrier. Maybe he thought she was afraid of him, and she wasn't. Maybe he still thought she was interested in him, and she wasn't. Tracey touched the front of her blouse. Her fingers stuck—the fabric was streaked with sweat and red dirt and the narcotic tar from the tobacco plants. She brushed at it and the smear became redder.

"Sure makes a mess, don't it, now? Good thing you weren't wearing nice shoes."

She glanced down at her old deck shoes, worn at the heels and coming apart at the seams, clown-spotted with yellow paint and dusted red. She swallowed the bubble in her throat, the pressure that might have been laughter or tears. The whole thing was coming apart.

"I guess you don't feel like I'll make a case out of this." She spoke carefully, as carefully as she placed her feet in the row, moving away.

Artis also moved just a little, and it might have been a swagger or that same tremor of the summer field. "What's to say? You took a tumble." Dragonflies worked back and forth, devil's darning needles, like those that buzzed over the pond behind that graying Ohio farmhouse. Her grandmother said that they did the devil's bidding to sew up the lips of lying children.

Tracey glanced up the field, to the Mexican laborers working their way back down the rows.

"They no habla, Ms. Gaines. And they won't." Artis shook out another cigarette and this time it seemed deliberate, a kind of punctuation. He hadn't smoked before, she knew.

Tracey turned and walked to the car, not allowing her hands to tremble or her eyes to glance his way. She couldn't control the flush in her face, but the sun covered that—she wouldn't allow him to gloat. It was only weakness that put her at his mercy, that old desire to please.

Dust had coated her car and clung to the leaves on the trees and the weeds in the ditch. She got in and closed the door even though heat blasted through the windshield and simmered on the black vinyl. She gripped the wheel and jerked away, burned. The air was thick. It was too hot to stay in the car and impossible to leave it—as she sat there, air conditioning blasting, Tracey replayed the conversation. The remark about the body shop. He knew. He knew about her car being keyed at school. It had been Jim who'd dug those long scratches into the paint, the day after Lakesha's death, and Artis knew. Approved, maybe even instigated. She was that close to going back and telling Artis all the rest of what she thought, the harsh things that she'd swallowed. In the rearview mirror, she saw Jim standing beside his father. He must have seen his father attack—no, Tracey couldn't say that—humiliate her. He gave her a hard-eyed stare.

She set the heels of her hands against the wheel. Wisdom or fear, one or both, kept her focused on the road as she eased away from the trucks.

CHAPTER TWELVE

Hunger and restlessness had overcome his reluctance to walk into Sports Central. Dave always felt conspicuous, even before the dragging sound of his steps made people cut their eyes away. He had a ragged feeling when alone among people—not the soothing solitude of reading among the library stacks or listening to music at home.

He took a booth near the back and ordered a beer and some Dragon Fire wings. The sports bar made no effort to attract a wide clientele. It was decorated in Carolina blue and white, with Saul County High's black and gold as punctuation. The menu cover featured Ramses sparring with an airborne dragon. The mascots of Southwest and Wysock Memorial High and the Cornerstone Academy were not represented, nor were those of Duke or Wake or the Wolfpack.

The waitress—class of 2001, she still wore the necklace—set down his plate and dropped a stack of paper napkins beside it. Dave watched stock cars circle on the television as he sucked peppery sauce from the wings.

One of the men at the bar began to laugh, and the joke spread from one to the next until even one guy separated from the rest joined late in the laughter. It renewed, like a ripple fading back, and then was done, the men absorbed once more in the race. Dave realized the lone man was Lester Cordwainer, so fat and slumped he seemed like some downhearted stranger and not the real estate broker who had been busily plowing old tobacco fields into bumper crops of tract housing. He must be sick, Dave thought, must be. He remembered the photo a year ago in the newspaper, Lester all teeth and expensive suit. They had graduated together, then Lester went a year to State before dropping out and coming home to make himself into a self-made man. He watched as Lester stared into a whiskey on the rocks and then downed it without pleasure, and felt a shudder of recognition.

Dave wiped the sauce from his fingers and considered the empty space across the table. He should have sat at the bar. The other booths were occupied by two or four, the even numbers of the regular world. Tracey was right, it seemed like everyone was coupled up. He wondered if she might spend an evening over beer and pretzels in a place like this, watching a ball game. Tried to picture her, but he kept seeing her on the porch of that old house, or plunging through the woods ahead of him. She probably didn't care for sports, or maybe only baseball. Some women liked baseball, the game played out on green grass, without violence. He liked baseball himself—even on TV, better in the stands. He had gotten hooked on the game early, when his father won the sales contest and a trip to Atlanta. He had been seven then, counting back. Seven or maybe eight. They drove down and saw the game from the box seats and stayed in a downtown hotel. He got a souvenir pennant and his father wore the baseball hat they put on him for the publicity photo, stubbornly wearing the thing for the entire game though it sat high on his curly hair. It was to be their only major league outing. When he moved to Baltimore, in the late summer before that winter, he went to several Orioles games, enchanted by the movement of white uniforms across the green turf, the intense light drenching the outfield as evening approached. Shadows swung across the field, the lights came up, and chimney swifts crisscrossed the beams. He'd never asked Tracey about sports—didn't know much about her, really. Maybe she liked football, being she was from Ohio. He always thought of James Wright's poem, young men in a game that foreshadowed the battering they would take for the rest of their lives.

The television announcer shouted and the men at the bar responded. Dave saw the wreck, with cars spinning across the track and others hitting them, each time a roar, and the smoke drifted and then there was fire licking at the underside of a car. The men leaned in.

"He's done," one said.

"Johnson bumped him."

"Nah, he got pushed hisself."

Silence as the yellow flag slowed everything to a procession and the crumpled cars were pulled away. It just renewed Dave's belief that NASCAR fans only watched for the wrecks, like the Romans for the moment some Gaul or Scythian fell and the gladius was thrust to his throat—the moment of potential, the blood under the skin ready for spilling.

Maybe not all the Romans, he thought. Maybe up in the seats a poet watched the way the shadow curved across the trampled sand from the sun dropping below the Colosseum parapet. He might turn from the games to study the line of flags along the rim, the summer sky darkening to blue from the stony white of noonday.

"Hey."

He was caught back by Lester's sudden presence at his table.

"Hey, Lester." The man stood there for a moment before Dave pointed toward the seat opposite. Lester sat down heavily.

"Davy Fordham." Lester put his hands flat on the table. "Where you been hiding?"

"I teach," he said. Not a profession for the country club.

"I build houses."

Dave tried again, remembering the Lester Cordwainer who wasn't 50 pounds overweight and sweating liquor. The one who was suicidally beautiful as he ran off-tackle against the oversized lines of Durham and Raleigh schools. "I'm at the alternative school. I see you have a new development just over on Ryman's Mill Road."

Lester coughed, "Cigarettes," and then nodded. "Yep, biggest one yet. Cluster homes—more to the acre."

"I read about that."

Lester seemed to be considering something out of place inside his chest. He pulled his hands back under the table and sat staring into the remains of Dave's food. The longer it went on, the more Dave wanted to slide away and leave him there. Maybe he was going to be sick.

"Lester ... you want something? Can I get you something?"

He looked stunned.

"You okay?"

Lester smiled, a slow spreading loose smile. The whites of his eyes were shot with blood vessels. "I'm way more'n okay, Davy. Making a bundle. More profit, you put the houses close together. Cluster homes, the latest thing. Yes, indeedy." He waved grandly at the wings congealing in their grease. "You go and finish up."

"I could get you a plate." The idea wasn't appealing.

"Nah. Nah. You see, I gotta get home. The wife ... and the kids." Lester winked, and the effect with that broad smile was terrible. "The wife. If she's back from her *afternoon*. And the kids, the junior Cordwainers." He shook his head and pressed his hand deep into the fat over his belt.

"How many kids do you have?"

Lester held up a fist and let one finger loose, then two, then three. "Two girls and a boy," he said. "A brood of vipers."

He must have seen the look on Dave's face, because he laughed and pushed himself to his feet. "Just a joke, son, a joke. Great kids. Three great kids. All at home. All of us, at home." He lurched to the door, his shoulders hunched as though he expected to face a stiff wind outside.

Dave let the waitress take the plate and bring another beer. Lester. Somewhere along the line he'd learned his woman was boring and his children demanding, and the ripples went back and forth, he was gone and she was lonely, she cheats and he drinks. Through the window Dave could see Lester sitting in his yellow Mercedes with the interior lights on. His head was back, his throat livid in the neon from the window signs. Then he bent forward, head bowed and resting on the steering wheel. Too drunk to drive? Dave hadn't thought so, just sick or weary, but by the time he thought to question it, Lester had roused himself and backed the car out onto the highway.

Dave remembered his father coming home, punctual, the time between the store closing and his arrival seldom varying by more than ten minutes. The arrival was frozen into ritual by memory, how his father put down his briefcase in the kitchen, kissed his mother, greeted Dave doing homework at the table. Then into the living room to read the afternoon *Post*, slowly. Other kids watched cartoons in the afternoon, but the TV set stayed dark until homework and the paper were both set aside, done. After dinner, his dad would change into work clothes to mow the lawn or trim hedges, or in bad weather disappear into his workshop out back, a refuge smelling of machine oil and plywood.

His father had died young—he had the bad luck to hit the last deer in a herd that crossed the road just before Grosvenor Bridge. The trailing buck was a big animal, and the farmer who ran from his fall plowing found his father already dead. He told everyone how he'd seen the deer, head-first into the car. When he got across the highway he found Mr. Fordham pinned to the seat by the buck's antlers, right through. Neither one was moving. People talked and talked about the accident, how strange to get killed when people ran into deer all the time. Bad luck, that was all. Dave was 12. He and his mother stayed on Bisher Street. And when he came home from Baltimore, it was to that house with green shutters. They had leaned on each other, his mother by then slowed with heart failure, and he a cripple. They were sustained, he supposed, by the familiarity of the house itself. Sometimes he drove past—the house wasn't out of the way, just a block off Elm. It was a shock when the new owners cut down all the flowering almonds and roses around the porch and finally lopped the pink crape myrtle back to a stump. The place looked bare without the trees and flowers. They had been his mother's—his father was always cutting and nailing, improving, while his mother planted and pruned—but Dave knew his father was proud of it all, sometimes stopping at the corner to look back at the place. Dave had seen him turn to look, and though he waved from his upstairs window his father never saw him.

I would have been a good father. Dave was sure of that—a better father because he would spend time with his son, to understand him. His father had been good to him but distant. Dave always realized that he was not as important as his mother, as the work and the workshop. There were depths to a boy that no one understood. Like Jim.

Things had changed with Jim. What had been shyness—the lefty's looping arm encircling his uneven writing—had turned to sullenness.

Whether it was the influence of the other boys, or the continuing problem over the dogs, or hormones—maybe all three—he couldn't say, but Jim was darker, stronger, and meaner. Suddenly he had muscles, his arms were lean and there was the shadow of a mustache.

Early in the semester, Dave had thought he was one of the kids who might escape back into the regular schools. He'd been getting Bs and Cs. He wasn't a discipline problem. Then Jim stopped turning in papers. He missed a test, then the makeup.

He gave Jim one more chance. On Friday, he was to have turned in three papers and an extra credit project that would take the place of the missed test. He showed up that afternoon with two papers, hastily written, each with the minimum number of words.

Dave read the papers carefully and turned them over on his desk. The air conditioning whirred in the vents. Jim was sitting off to the side, head on his arm, appearing to sleep.

"Jim."

He made a production of stirring, stretching, sitting up.

"I appreciate the work you've done to complete these papers," he said.

"Did I pass?"

"...Mr. Fordham."

"Did I pass, Mr. Fordham," he dutifully repeated.

"You have passing marks on these papers. But you needed three papers, and the extra credit work."

"I didn't have enough time," he muttered.

Dave nodded. "It was a lot of work, but it was your opportunity to catch up for the semester. Since you are short two grades, you will have to take the final exam."

"That's not fair! I was only absent twice!"

"That's not the issue, Jim." He kept his voice low and controlled. "Your attendance is fine, but you also need to complete all assigned work with a passing grade to be exempt from the final."

"It's because of *her*."

"You have to take the final because of your grade record. It's not so bad—you'll pass easily, if you prepare."

"No friggin' way." Jim enunciated each word, set them before Dave as a challenge. Cursing a teacher could get him suspended. He was tense, his arms straight on the desk, his hands almost tightened into fists. He has his father's eyes, Dave thought. The intensity, even if they were brown.

Dave got up and walked casually toward the door. He needed to put space between them, and the shadows on the frosted glass window of people passing in the hall was a reminder he wasn't alone here. "Let's stick with standard English, okay? Now, I understand you are upset about having to take the finals, but that's the rule. Let's go back to the time issue. Do you want to talk about that?"

Jim shrugged.

"Are you working?" Tracey had told him he was out in the fields, and he could see that in his spring sunburn.

"On the farm. You know."

"Do you work at night, or on the weekends? If it's affecting your school work, maybe you should talk with your dad about it."

"It's not my dad. It's not because of the farm." His face worked, muscles in his jaw clenching on something.

"You're a lot of help to your dad."

"You don't know!" Jim burst out. "My dad has all these problems because of her. We shouldn't even be living out here in the sticks. Everything would be great except for her."

The mother. Dave had heard the reports. The mother had flaunted a very public affair that drove Artis Pennell out of business and out of Charlotte. No wonder the boy was so angry.

"Jim," he said, trying to find the right words. "What happened with your mother should not…"

"Don't talk about my mother!" Jim glowered, seeming to gain size and strength as he gripped the edges of his desk.

"I don't want to talk about her. I want to talk about you."

"It's not her. It's that old bi—broad—Gaines."

Dave tried not to let the shock come through, but Jim wasn't looking at him anyway. He pushed out of his desk and began to walk around the back of the room, pausing to stare at the pictures of presidents, at the map of the world. His shoulders sloped with new muscle.

"She hates me. She hates my dad and she hates me. She shouldn't be allowed to cause trouble."

"Ms. Gaines doesn't hate anyone." Dave tried to gauge if this was a real threat or just adolescent posturing. "We have rules we must abide by in our classes, just like you."

Jim got up and went to the bookshelves, picked up one of the encyclopedia volumes and began to flip the pages back and forth.

"Your father is proud of you, Jim. I saw that when I talked with him on Parents' Night."

Jim tossed the book onto the shelves, knocking another one off. He picked it up and set it back, taking the time to align them spine to spine. "I'm just one more thing for him." Jim pushed the hair away from his face, for a moment appearing much younger.

"You can help him by doing well in school."

"We don't need any help. We manage. My dad doesn't need help and neither do I." Jim flung his hand out, nearly to the books he'd just stacked.

"Jim ..."

"Just let me go. Let me be." Jim was at the door, just that quick, standing and waiting. Dave tried to read him but the signals were jumbled, boy and man, angry teen and hurt child. He could take him down to the office. Dave opened the door, reminded Jim about the test schedule, and got nothing in response. He watched him lope down the hall. Was this decision any better than the one he'd made with Trey? Or had he let Jim off too lightly?

"Another?" He looked up, trying to place the voice. The waitress swung her head away at the roar as the race ended, and her thick black hair moved and fell back. A former student, but something else.

The winning car spun its tires in the infield. Smoke covered the track, the stands. The final results were posted, Chevy, Chevy, Ford.

It was the way she moved, that's what caught his eye. Not the hair. The way she listened by bending her head down and a little to the side, a tilt that made her hair fall against her cheek on one side and away from her face on the other. It reminded him of Randi Wohlberg. Just before they broke up she had cut her hair, and that showed a different side of her. She began to tilt her head when she listened to him, a little questioning. They connected the last year of graduate school when both of them were so intent on getting out that they could hardly see each other. Randi went to San Diego, or

San Antonio, he couldn't remember, and they had quickly lost touch. He tried to imagine where she was, her life, how she'd made it, but he could just as easily imagine her waiting on tables like Class of 2001, or disappearing into the city as he did. For a while.

The waitress dropped the check on his table and he covered it with a ten.

He drove home the usual way, past the closed shops on Virginia Street, past the glowing excess of the CVS pharmacy that had replaced them. Pine, Maple, Elm. The lights were on in his old home on the corner of Bisher. If he didn't look too close it might be the same place, it might be the Fordham house, with Mom reading in the living room with her feet up, and Dad in the workshop.

So easy to take the physical for the emotional, the symbol to stand for what isn't there any longer. He turned into the duplex and parked in the assigned place around back, climbed the stairs to 2-A, opened the door and remembered that his father once had painted the sunroom yellow, just like his kitchen. Tracey had spilled yellow paint on the ladder when she was helping him and had been so apologetic, wadding up paper towel after paper towel as she tried to get it clean, and he laughed and pointed out that the ladder was covered with old paint. Finally he took the roll of paper towels away—"A tree thanks me"—and she picked up her brush and dabbed his hand with it. He felt an immediate heat, looked at her and the moment roared—then she headed back up the ladder. Hot and cold, hot and cold. Dave stood there and remembered the lines about indecision.

He set his bag on the kitchen counter and looked at the brightness of the room, now warm and welcoming. It was nice of her to come and help him. But she was as tough to read as Jim, and as tough to reach. It was all a mess. He wished she wasn't tangled up with this Artis thing, the dogs, the girl, the connection between them that made him twinge.

Dave turned on the light in his bedroom. The little paper umbrella he'd brought back from their dinner in Raleigh sat cockeyed in the ivy plant. Bright pink. He remembered how it spun around the rim of her drink.

CHAPTER THIRTEEN

Tracey squeezed another few cents' worth into the tank, $15.75.

She threaded her way past the racks of chips and cookies to the single cash register, where three women were huddled with Jenny McAndrews, who clerked there afternoons and weekends.

Jenny glanced up, and her face lost all animation. "Hello, Miz Gaines."

The women turned, the black woman vaguely familiar, the others strangers, but they looked at her as though they knew her.

"Fifteen seventy-five," she said, reaching a twenty toward the clerk.

A pile of the latest *Saul County Citizen* occupied the counter, its ornate Gothic masthead taking up a good part of the front page. And right beneath it, "Dog Owner Indicted in Death of County Child." Under that, her picture and Artis's nestled side by side in the middle of the columns of type.

She stared at the paper, for a moment part of that circle of silent women. Her picture was a little out of focus, taken by the student photographer for the yearbook. "Our New Faculty!!" Now it was crossed with a plaid pattern, as though seen through a window screen. The picture of Artis looked like it had been scissored out of a family photograph, with a piece of a building behind his head. There was nothing to link them, two strangers whose photos had landed side by side. The story pressed them close together—she caught a phrase here and there, "witnessed the attack," "local farmer," "trial set for district court."

"You didn't give that child a lick of help when she needed it. What good you think *this* is?" The black woman jabbed her finger into the pile of papers. The others said nothing, but their eyes agreed.

"I'm sorry," she said, words that came too easily.

"Sorry, I guess so. Who you think you are, anyway?" The woman set her shoulders back. "You the lady of the house, all to yourself. La-ti-da. Let that child die, yes you did."

The twenty trembled where she held it. Tracey dropped it on the counter. The clerk rang up the sale, not saying a word, not looking up.

"I'll take a paper, too."

The background music jingled happily, something country. A cooler motor kicked on. The register opened and Jenny handed her the change. Tracey lifted a paper from the stack and headed for the door.

"Some folks just gotta push things." A different voice. "Not enough to ruin one family, gotta hurt another one."

She turned back. The shortest woman still had her mouth open; her doughy face was blotched red.

"If you mean telling the truth. If you mean doing what I'm supposed to do."

Confronted, the woman didn't answer, but Tracey heard her say, as she went out, "Leastways he's one of *us*."

"Hmmmph!" That was the black woman.

Now she recognized her, one of Lakesha's relatives. At the funeral she wore a black hat with a blue flower, and was right behind Orenna when the mother unleashed that look.

Tracey pulled off at the Ruritan picnic area, behind the lone table and under the shade of the pine trees. Feels right, she thought. I'm a tourist here. An interloper. The white house drew her—head for home, for the security of her own front porch—but she wasn't turning around because of three millworkers at a convenience store. She turned down the radio and unfolded the paper, oddly oversized, like one of the old city papers, but thin.

"The tragic death of little Lakesha Sipe, this past March near her home on Burnt Cabin Road, will soon come before the courts," she read. "The Saul County grand jury has returned a true bill of indictment against Artis Pennell, 44, of Eccelston Road, charging him with involuntary manslaughter, permitting dogs to run at large after dark, and harboring vicious dogs."

She didn't realize he was as old as that.

"District Attorney Ervin Dupree said he was pleased at the action of the grand jury on this case and another high-profile crime considered by the panel, the brutal murder of Mrs. Emily Sturgis in her home for $23 in cash."

Tracey remembered the widow beaten to death in her trailer for that little sum of money and her car. Two young thugs from Richmond were arrested months after the murder, when they were stupid enough to return to Saul County in the same car with stolen Virginia plates.

"Pennell, a local tobacco farmer, has maintained that his dogs were not involved in the attack. They remain in custody at the county animal shelter. The case is expected to hinge on the testimony of Miss Tracey Gaines, who witnessed the attack. Efforts to reach either party for comment were unsuccessful at press time."

She tossed the paper on the passenger side. Now she wished she hadn't gone to the trouble to get a new number, unlisted. Mike Keener surely would have called, warned her about the story and the picture. Only the school had her new number, and Dave, and her scraps of distant family. Still, he could have come to the house—he'd had gall enough to do it before.

Tracey pulled around the table and then, seeing an old pickup truck wallowing down the road, gunned the car and bounced out of the picnic area in a spray of dirt and gravel. The truck driver honked at her, a reproachful beep-beep, and she flipped him the finger.

She didn't think he'd been going that fast, but the truck kept pace with her now, one fender bouncing where it had rusted free of its lower moorings. It was 55 through here and she pushed it to 65. The truck stayed close behind.

With the glare of the sun, she'd barely seen the man, someone in a baseball cap, an impression of a long white face. Tracey kept driving. She thought about pulling off but no place seemed safe, the side roads deserted, not a gas station or roadside market. And if she did pull off, was that any better? She wondered if he had a gun. A statistic, three out of ten cars had a gun in them. Three out of five? No telling, down here. And the politeness that smoothed every social surface covered all sorts of murky emotions. The road went into a patch of woods, the sun cut off, dark. The man behind her was visible now, a grizzled face under a baseball cap. The worn black pickup had a TOYOTA bug shield on the front. Was he going to follow her until she stopped?

Tracey realized that she had slid down in her seat. *Less of a target, then.* Seeing the young men leaving the school, slumped almost out of sight as they imitated thug life videos. She straightened and gripped the wheel.

She slowed up and the truck did, too. Tracey decided that if he turned off when she did, she would not follow the route to Gloria's place. No sense taking this to her, though she could imagine the Jersey girl coping. She'd keep driving on that road—what road? Whetstone. It came out on Storey Mill, and there was a convenience store, a telephone. *Too stubborn to get a cellphone.* She wondered again if he had a gun. In the rearview mirror he was just the same, driving, no gestures, no effort to pass. She couldn't see any gun rack but it was a pistol she feared.

Open fields. Sun glared from his windshield. She wished she could see his face as the four-way stop appeared, Whetstone Road crossing the highway. Tracey slowed but didn't stop, didn't signal, turned left and willed herself not to be caught looking. The pickup went straight through. She saw his face turned towards her as he kept going, and Tracey let out a sigh.

Nothing to it, she thought. Nothing to fear.

She picked up the notebook paper where she'd written out the directions, translated from the tiny spiral Gloria had drawn on the back of her business card. Left off 93 onto Whetstone Road. Go about four miles.

Her stomach churned. It was supposed to be a nice afternoon. Go see Gloria's place after a couple of heartfelt invitations, come back through Shawton to have dinner with Dave. She shivered instead with cold-chill memories, the bus lumbering away, the dogs, the late winter sky, the shock of red when her fingers lifted blood into the headlight beams.

Left on Poplar Level Road. Two miles. The roads were narrow and unfamiliar. Farmhouses, fields, trailers, old log tobacco barns held together with kudzu and recycled metal signs from gas stations.

The deposition had knotted her thoughts for days. Was she sure she had told everything? Told everything right? And now there would be a trial.

Left on Catawba Road. The pavement ended. The farm road was a single gravel lane. She passed a gated driveway and then an area that had been logged and left with a few desolate trees amid the stumps and brush. Finally there was a farm house and two mailboxes, one with Proctor painted on it. A rusty sign EGGS was stuck in the ditch. A pretty painted-wood sign for Gold Hill Apiaries swung between white posts in the yard.

The farmhouse was swaybacked, with a screen porch on one side and a rusty oil tank on the other. It made her think of another place where they used to get eggs, one of Carl's "shirttail relatives," a second cousin or cousin once removed. Wesley had a garden and sold vegetables and eggs. Once she had gone there and he had come out to meet her with a dead chicken in one hand, bloody, its neck truncated above his gnarled grip. "Havin' me some chicken tonight," he said, with a lopsided grin. "Wa'nt planning on it, not being Sunday or comp'ny or anything, but the chickens decided otherwise." She imagined a dog, or maybe the chicken escaping into the road, though cars passed infrequently. What had happened? "Bought some new birds, thought they was enough of 'em. Put 'em in with the others. This one, they didn't like." He put eggs into the tray she'd returned, his hands cradling them one by one lest arthritis make him fumble. "You heard tell of pecking order? That's from chickens. They go after one that's differ'nt, or sick, or hurt. I guess this one might have had some blood on it from the cage, some reason, and they pecked at it. Pecked it to death." Tracey could still see his sly old face, dirt creased in the wrinkles as it had been in his shirt and overalls.

The farm road was mostly ruts, slow going for her Honda. She found a place to park that didn't seem to be in anyone's way.

An old man came around the barn and she half expected to see a chicken dangling from his fist. Instead, he carried two wire baskets full of eggs.

"Morning, ma'am. You need eggs?" He was the egg man from the farmer's market, the one set up beside the honey stand.

"Hi. I'm here to see Gloria?"

He looked disappointed. "She's yonder, at her work." He lifted his furrowed chin toward a shed that had new windows in its old walls.

"She invited me to visit."

"Well, then, you're welcome." The whole expression of his face altered, opening up. "We're right glad to see you….Miss …"

"Tracey," she said. "Tracey Gaines."

"Harley Proctor." He patted her on the shoulder and urged her toward the shed. "You go on, she's inside."

She walked past the chicken run—the dusty earth, remembered smell of mash and litter—and found the door of the shed ajar. It was painted with bees and flowers like the sign by the road.

Gloria was seated on a tall stool. Her blond hair was pulled back into a single thick braid. A box of labels rested in front of her and others, completed, were scattered around the table. She leaned close to her work with a calligrapher's pen and ink.

Tracey tapped on the door frame. Gloria lifted the pen and glanced over her shoulder.

"Tracey! I didn't think you'd ever come see us." She turned around and pulled another stool over. "Have a sit."

"Thanks. You said any weekday afternoon."

"I meant it. We're always around here, once we've hit the markets."

They both used "we" effortlessly, like a married couple. Tracey wondered about their relationship, this woman younger than she, and a man at least 70. It wasn't something you could ask. Tracey leaned across and read the labels—Sourwood, Poplar, Taste of Spring, Wild Flower—elegant script filling the space between the flowered border and a printed business address.

"You make so many kinds?"

"The bees do. We just collect it." Gloria pointed out the different colors of honey in the bottles displayed around the shed, amber and golden. "Sourwood and Poplar are the two easiest, they bloom reliably and there are a lot of trees around the hives. Wild Flower covers summer and fall, field flowers, and Taste of Spring has a lot of tree bloom and clover in it. I'll show you the hives, if you want."

Tracey still wondered how you could tell where thousands of bees had foraged, enough to put a name to it. Would the bees sting her if she went near the hives, not recognizing her? "I've never been around bees."

"They won't know if you don't tell 'em."

"How'd you learn all this?" She motioned around the room—the charts of bee diseases, books, boxes of honey, devices that she had no name for, blocks of dull golden wax stacked like bullion.

"Harley's wife, before she died. I used to sell handmade jewelry in the booth next to them at the Tri-County market on Sundays. When Angelo headed to the West Coast, I decided to learn something useful." Tracey could hear how she used lightness to soften the reality of that abandonment.

Gloria stacked the finished labels. "Let's have some coffee—you drink coffee? Or tea?"

"Either."

They found the old man in the kitchen, sorting washed eggs into recycled cartons from Winn-Dixie and Bi-Lo. Brown eggs went to one side, white ones to the other.

"Folks think they's a difference," he explained. "Eggs is eggs, just different chickens laying 'em."

"You want some coffee with us?"

He nodded and stayed at his sorting. Tracey sat down at the kitchen table, a familiar thing in its scars and scratches, mismatched wooden chairs around it. The kitchen had wooden cupboards that reached all the way to the high ceiling—a stepstool beside the refrigerator was more than an occasional help. Gloria pulled a can of coffee from one shelf, bottled water from another. Heavy rust stains in the deep enameled sink showed why.

"Mr. Proctor."

"Harley, or I'll ma'am you right back," he warned.

"Harley—I live on the other side of the county, near Taberville. The graveyard at my house has Proctors buried in it."

"Yeah, them's my people. Gloria told me you bought the Floyd place. All the Proctors hereabouts are related, most of all the dead ones."

"I wondered."

"More of us underground than above, these days," he said. "That's how Gloria come to be here—I imagine you was speculating."

Tracey tilted her head, not wanting to admit yes or no.

"All Mary's doing." He closed the lid on the final dozen and pulled out a chair opposite. Gloria came and put down spoons and sugar and milk. "We only had the one girl, and she married and moved away. Not much other family, no one that wanted the farm—leastways to be a farm. You see how it is. The old people die and the young ones sell off the place in lots."

Tracey nodded, thinking of the tract she passed with rows of modular homes set square along treeless streets, a step up from a trailer park.

"The women, they yakked it up every market. Gardens and canning and quilts, all such stuff. Gloria came around to learn about the bees."

"And Mary read about this stewardship program," Gloria cut in, as she poured coffee. "It matches landowners with younger people who don't have property but want to farm."

"She agreed to take over the place and keep it in farming, then pass it on. Moved in the spare room and that come to be a godsend, when Mary took ill."

"I took over the hives while she could still teach me."

"And she told Mary she'd see to me, make sure I didn't go to wrack and ruin on my own." Harley spooned sugar into his cup, three times, and stirred hard, clanking the spoon round and around. "You ever farm any?"

The question took her by surprise, her thoughts still on how Gloria came to the farm. "My grandparents. My grandfather raised Herefords."

"Used to run cattle, 'fore it got so's I couldn't put up hay and couldn't buy help."

"Your grandmother?" Gloria asked.

"I helped her with the gardening and the canning. I stayed there a lot when I was a kid."

"I love to can."

"Me, too," Tracey said, and realized she did. She remembered the snapped beans and cut corn, blackberries, tomatoes, jellies. Mostly she remembered sliding scalded peaches from their skins, the thick smell of fruit. The bite of the fruit acids on her hands, knife-nicked, skinned by the pits. Syrup steaming in the pan, poured over the halves, the quarts golden and hot under a towel.

"They had a beautiful farm. In Ohio. The ground was just rolling a bit, like around here. Everything was neat—my grandfather could never stand how some farmers let their fences go and left their implements out in the fields to rust."

"Sounds like you loved the place."

"I stayed there a lot. Summers. My grandfather died and once Grandma was alone, I spent weekends and helped her out."

Harley nodded vigorously. "That's right. You must have been a big help to her. Now, my girl is off in Texas and scarce brings the grandbabies once a year. They don't know about the home place, don't lift a hand when they visit."

"I didn't do so much." Tracey avoided his sharp eyes. "Grandma rented out the fields and we just had the garden then and some fruit trees. She took care of it all until she got sick."

"And then you took care of her."

Tracey put down her cup and stared into it. She had a momentary vision of her grandmother, leaning against the newel post to catch her breath. She was fifteen that summer.

"Is she still there?" Gloria's smooth forehead wrinkled with concern.

"No. She die—passed." Tracey felt the words shift in her mouth, the hard word for the gentle one, the plain fact for the hope.

"She taught you a lot, I can tell," Harley said after a minute.

"She did." So easy to talk and talk, they were so open with their stories here, all the details of their lives, and before she knew it she was that close to the painful memories.

"My grandmother worked in a factory, so I never learned much except about overtime and unions from her," Gloria said.

"Bless her soul," Harley said, reflexively.

"Funny. I think about planting corn in the garden." Tracey remembered the crumbly soil and the seeds dyed pink with fungicide. "She hoed up the hills and flattened them on top. She taught me to count out the seeds. One for the worm and one for the crow, one for the weather and one to grow. And then one more."

"Ain't that just like a woman." Harley clucked at the idea.

"What about the moon signs?" Gloria challenged.

"That's science, not witching."

Tracey stared at the marks cut into the table, knife-cuts from making meals, jabs and curlicues of children's mischief. You could find patterns there, meaning maybe, like in the seeds planted. She saw women huddled over such things—the women in the store, the paper like the opened lives of some creature under their examination.

CHAPTER FOURTEEN

Hello." Dave almost hung up at the lack of response, the strange mechanical buzzing. "Hello?" He waited, watching a woman tug a fat spaniel along the sidewalk across the street. "Hello?"

"Dave. Thank God you're there, Dave." Her voice, wavering between fear and anger. "Please."

"Tracey? What is it?"

"Just come. Now."

"Tracey?"

"Can't—no, stop it, just stop!" The buzzing became a mechanical roar, a chain saw? Motorcycle? "Dave, please."

The phone clicked and there was only silence.

He ignored the muscle spasms as he hurried down the steps, tried to ignore the knot in his stomach. She needed him. Whatever was out there—he almost threw up. Whatever it was, he wasn't ready for.

Back street to back street, avoiding the traffic lights on the main drag, wheeling around an old lady going 15, running a red light.

Why did she live out there alone? No one could see her house from the highway, or anything but the roofline from the trailer park. He had a vision of Artis getting out of his truck, Artis pulling a rifle from the rack in the back window.

He bent at the pain, again, like a stick was twisting his innards.

The car skidded around a turn, the back end sliding out of his control; he felt the wetness between his palms and the wheel, then disused reflexes took hold, eyes flicking to the rearview mirror as he grabbed the inside of every curve. The four-cylinder complained and he thought momentarily about the miles on the car. Tracey needed him. He went onto the mushy shoulder and almost off the road to avoid a tractor hauling a spray rig.

The blue house, green fields, the trailer park sign—poor Lakesha—the narrow opening to Tracey's lane. The car bottomed out as he bumped along the ruts, the trees so thick it was like driving into a tunnel.

Tracey's car sat placidly in the sun. No other car. Nothing to see under the sun.

He left the engine running as he step-dragged to the porch. "Tracey!" He tried the handle—locked—and hammered on the door. He smelled burned oil. Off in the distance, chain saws or motorbikes whined. He shifted his foot in the damnable brace and leaned to knock again.

The door pulled away from his fist. Tracey stood there, her eyes showing white all around like a spooked horse, holding her place with one hand on the door, the other on the frame.

"Dave," his name on a whoosh of released breath. He saw her stomach rising and falling under the flowered sundress.

"What's the matter?" He put his hand on her bare arm and felt her flinch, then ease.

"Oh, God." She swung the door back and let him in. "I think they're gone."

"Who? Artis? Who was here?"

"Kids—just some kids." Tracey hung her head; hair shielded her face. "They were riding around and around the house on four-wheelers. I couldn't get them to stop."

"Did you call the cops?"

She shook her head. Her hair shifted back and forth, catching the light, red over brown. He almost forgot what had brought him.

Four-wheelers buzzed like a nest of hornets inside a wall.

"They're coming back."

Dave looked at the yard and saw, now, the tire tracks and places where dirt had been torn up, red clay through the thin grass. A branch had been pulled off one of the bushes.

He walked out on the porch. The buzzing turned into snarling engine noise. There must be four or five of them coming up the lane that went to the graveyard. They went behind the house and then roared around the corner, four boys on mud-spattered machines, standing on the pegs, whooping and yelling. The first one saw his Escort parked right across the path, and turned away from it, toward the house, looking up and catching his eye, waving to warn the others who didn't yet realize what was happening.

The first one leaped his ATV past the shed and across the drive, toward the band of pine trees. The second one followed. The third one, on a John Deere, was Jim Pennell. They ran follow-the-leader through the trees and down to the trailer park road, over the tobacco fields and gone.

They left a smell of metal and oil smoke and raw dirt.

Dave stared after them. Jim had been wearing that familiar blue plaid shirt. He didn't have a helmet, just a ball cap, and he'd looked right at him. Without reaction, without fear. They knew he couldn't do anything, anything other than be a witness. He wished he could run them down and drag them off their hornet-bikes, throw them down and pummel sense into their empty heads. Crazy.

The afternoon quieted. A bird called, three notes repeated. Dave waited. It was so unreal, like a movie set empty of actors.

"Dave?"

Tracey came out and stood beside him. She held her hands folded together but he saw a tremor.

"They're gone."

"You ran them off."

He laughed at the idea. "They didn't like having anyone else see them."

"I'm sorry—I didn't mean to drag you out here."

Dave looked at her eyes on a level with his own, hair he still wanted to touch. "I'm glad you called," he said, too flat for what he felt. "You sounded scared to death."

"Yeah, well."

"Let's sit down for a minute. You want something to drink? Coffee? Iced tea? Something stronger?"

"A slug of scotch might be right."

"Really?"

"Like you don't think I have anything in the house but tea?"

He would have thought white wine, if anything, in her tall kitchen cabinets.

"No, really, coffee," she said.

"Coffee." She followed him inside, sat down at the kitchen table and put her hands together on it. He had a strange moment of watching her watch him as he moved around, as though this were his kitchen and not a place he'd visited a few times. With her directions he found the coffee filters and a spoon for the coffee. The water hissed as it began to drop into the stained pot.

"I heard them this morning," she began, waving generally in the direction of the woods. "They're around, on the farm roads and even the main roads sometimes, but they've never bothered. I don't know what got them started."

He wondered if she had recognized Jim. She didn't mention him. Maybe that's why she hadn't called the police, not wanting another confrontation with the Pennells, or maybe even thinking about him and his fool investment in that kid. He'd talked so much about Jim and his hopes that he would make it.

She got up and poured the coffee into mismatched mugs, one from a bank in Ohio. She added milk and sugar to his, milk only to hers.

"Sorry I don't have cream."

"Haven't touched the stuff in years."

Tracey held her cup in both hands, the way his uncle had when Parkinson's set in and he couldn't trust them to be steady. She had slender wrists, more elegant than powerful.

"This isn't the first time, is it?"

"This? Yes, in fact, it is."

"But there've been other things."

"Yes, oh yes." She laughed, twisted the cup around in her hands and seemed to focus on the bank logo, fading and blurred. "I was never sure. Some vandalism. Maybe a little paranoia creeping in. And the snide remarks and looks from people I don't even know. God, I hate to think of going back to school—they've had all summer to work the topic over."

Dave was glad she hadn't heard the things he had. Sometimes people just wanted to get a rise out of you. He didn't usually oblige, but knew that school would bring it all back. He understood how kids who were bullied felt, their shoulders hunched up from the moment they got on the bus, waiting for it to start. It was different from his own particular shame. Similar, but different.

Tracey got up and moved around the kitchen, straightening a picture, poking a finger into the dirt under an asparagus fern. The sundress was faded and soft, pulled close to her body by a tie in the front that swung when she turned, circling back to take the coffee pot and refill their cups. She left hers sitting, untouched, and began another nervous circuit of the room. She opened the refrigerator and stalled there, hidden behind the door, then began moving things around, opening drawers and rattling plastic.

"You want to stay for dinner?" She popped her head up over the door, eyebrows arched hopefully. "It's just potluck."

"That would be great. But we could go out somewhere."

She shook her head and plunged back into the refrigerator. "Salad. Cheesecake. I have spaghetti left over."

"That's always better the second night."

She stood up. The nervousness that tightened her face began to slip away.

Dave started to help but Tracey demanded he sit still. She pulled out a pot of spaghetti—"I always make a bunch at one time," she admitted—and set it on the stove to start heating. The lettuce was the kind that came in a bag, pre-washed and chopped, but she added tomatoes and green peppers and black olives. (He could move them to the side of the bowl.)

She began to hum as she worked, setting the table, pulling out a covered pot of honey and another that held butter. She sliced bread, thick, and arranged the slices in a basket lined with a yellow dishtowel.

Dave heard sizzling and went to the stove. The spaghetti was sticking and he added a little water, stirred. It smelled of garlic and parmesan, and that deep tomato aroma that only comes when the pasta has been allowed to sit and then brought back to warmth. He laid the spoon in a spoon rest his grandmother might have used,

Blue Willow. He hadn't thought he was hungry until the kitchen filled with steam and the smell of herbs. She held the plates while he lifted helpings of spaghetti between a spoon and fork. He shook the dressing and she turned off the overhead light, turned on the single bulb under a stenciled lampshade. For a moment, Dave found himself in a place he remembered from a distance but had never been.

Over dinner, they talked about whether magnolias smelled good or not, road work that had taken a line of lofty willow oaks, the dour Amish neighbors she'd known in Ohio. There were Mennonites here, he told her: "Drive up near Robeyville and you might see some of them riding bicycles. They wear light blue and the women have the little white caps with the strings flying in the breeze."

The cheesecake, he was surprised to see, was homemade. The slices were dense and crumbly, and he admired the talent that went into creating it.

"Actually, it's easier than pie or cake." Tracey scraped at the graham cracker edge. "I indulge myself, now and again."

"It's incredible," he said, and meant it.

Tracey was carrying the plates to the sink when a truck blew its air horn out on the road. She startled and the forks clattered to the floor. The dishes rattled as she put them in the sink. "Sheesh." She bent and picked up the silverware.

"Maybe something in the road."

"I'm jumpy, I know it." She wiped her hands and stood leaning against the sink. "I keep having this awful dream—not the same dream, but versions of it." Tracey closed her eyes, breathed deeply. He remembered her stomach rising and falling with panicked breaths, the shuddering that went through her. There was more to this, not just kids. Not just the nightmares she wouldn't share. Although she'd pulled away from him in the past, Dave said it anyway. "I should stay the night, in case they come back." What would he do? He didn't know, but he thought he could do something.

She didn't answer that, but she did ask him to sit for a while "and digest."

Warm evening light filtered into the living room, moving with the wind in the trees. She'd put no curtains to the high, arched windows, but the interior shutters had been repaired and were hooked back with new hardware. What a strange mixture, a rec room sofa covered in scratchy plaid, a Victorian armchair, a leather ottoman. Jazz played from a stereo old enough to have a turntable, but there was no television. Small crocks and chipped plates filled a bow-fronted china closet. He thought he could figure some of it out, the simplicity of the enforced single, moving what needs to be moved, less each time. Remnants of the marriage mixed with the things she had dug up, the old, the broken, the antique. It made him think of Thoreau, that wonderful fraud. Instead of seeking independence in a bare shack (but taking his wash and mending home to mom), she was getting away from the bareness of her life by wrapping herself in a comforting quilt of the discarded, broken, reused, useless.

He sat at his end of the sofa and she curled at the other, sandals kicked off and bare feet tucked under her.

The instrumental segued into a torch song, "Come rain or come shine." Dave considered the antique photos in tiger-patterned frames, stolid women in high-collared dresses. Bombazine? He always wondered what that looked like, maybe that half-shiny black. One man, leaning on a cane, had a huge mustache and deep-set eyes. "He looks like a formidable old gent," he said, over the singer's aching lament.

"Flea market." He glanced at her, caught a rueful mouth before she turned it into a grin. "Yeah, really. Just like digging out back. I love the old things, and it doesn't really matter if that's my great-granddad or not, I can look at old Hezekiah and think about his life."

Dave thought of the tintypes on the shelf over his computer, not purchased but real, his ancestors with pistols carried at chest level, rakish cavalry hats with plumes, the loops of braid stiff on their new uniforms. You had to tilt them against the light to see them properly, to look at faces that hadn't survived Chickamauga but left a baby or two to carry on the cleft Pettigrew chin. It made him nervous that she assembled the trappings of family so casually. He got up and went to the photos, looked closely at them. The mustachioed man wore a Masonic ring.

Between the windows, a pump shotgun rested on a pair of coat hooks. "I don't think you dug this up."

"My father. He said I should have something in the house for protection, living way out there. Back in Pennsylvania. I could never imagine using the thing."

"You know how?"

"Yes, I do." She sounded stern, as though he had questioned some basic ability. "I wonder what their faces would have looked like, if I'd come out on the porch carrying that." She shook her head. "But they're just kids."

But there's more to this than kids.

"Do you have shells for it?"

"Dad made me take a few. They're in the hutch, if you have to know, and I bet you were ready to ask."

That sounded more like Tracey. Dave tried not to smile. He pulled the drawer open and saw half a dozen shells rolling around the back—he picked one up and saw it was double-ought buckshot, 12 gauge. *Daddy wasn't playing.* He tossed it in the drawer and went back to his corner of the sofa.

"He hunted a little. I never did, but he taught me how to load and fire a shotgun. I didn't hurt his feelings and tell him I didn't plan to ever do it again."

Their cultures were about a generation off. Her father had treated guns as leisure instruments. His father thought of guns as tools rather than playthings. They had pistols for target shooting, .22s for plinking, shotguns for skeet, .30-06s for deer hunting. Dave had learned to use them all, with respect and care.

"I think he was scared to death for me. He asked me to move home, after the divorce, but I couldn't do that. It was bad enough visiting. I stayed for a year out on that farm in Venango County, struggling along so I could show myself I could do it. Maybe to show Carl, I don't know."

"He didn't think you could?"

"Just being stubborn, or macho, or something. The place was his idea."

"But you like the country."

"I wasn't ready to, then. I was still grieving over my grandmother."

"But it's okay now."

"It's okay—here." She seemed to hold her breath.

"They say the time comes when you can go back to those places without it hurting. It's true, I guess, but the problem is when."

"So have you gotten to that point yet?" Tracey was suddenly intent, the lines deepening between her brows. "Can you go back there?"

"I'm like you: It's okay—here."

"At least you were able to come home again."

"Yeah, something like that." Dave thought that wasn't any accomplishment, to crawl back to the place you'd left on two feet.

"And you're teaching. That had to be hard, to go back in front of a bunch of kids."

He saw Trey, and the others, the sullen faces, the waiting anger, the dark street, the melting slush running into his shoes and then pain, white-hot.

"You were quite a different person before you went to Baltimore," she said, even more gently.

Sure. He remembered himself like a man in a dungeon remembers sunshine. What could he tell her? That he'd been quick and strong, maybe no great athlete but sure of himself? Sure on his feet. Dave felt his toes draw in on the wounded foot, cramping as though in response. At least you still have a foot, the doctor had said.

"Today," he started, then began again. "When I was driving, today. I used to love my cars, but now I don't drive except what I have to. I had a red Camaro, when I was in college—but today, it was like I was back then, I started to like the speed and skidding around the turns. Once I even reached for the clutch."

He saw what she must see, a balding cripple in a little teal-green Ford, and felt the warmth creep up his neck.

"I couldn't believe it was you when I heard the car. You must have broken every speed limit."

"A few."

"Thanks." She reached across the space between them and took his hand. He gripped hers back, too hard, then relaxed. "It was hard to call."

"You shouldn't think twice."

"I thought more than twice. It's hard for me, Dave. I'm used to doing for myself."

Her head was turned away. Maybe she was studying the way the light had gone so quickly, the trees around the house pulled like curtains against the sunset. Dave looked past her to the office room, with its desk and the green eye of the computer, and the spill of brightness from the kitchen. When she turned back, her eyes were wide—not innocent, but wary, like an animal straining to sense what waited.

"I used to be different, too," she said. "More trusting. When Carl left it was so unexpected. I kept trying to figure out where things had changed, how I had missed so much. It made me doubt everything about myself and everyone around me."

"Maybe it wasn't you at all."

"It took me a while, but I finally realized that. He changed. We both did, but him more. But Carl was a good human being, so he tried to hide it, and not hurt me. That was worse."

Did he betray her? Dave thought he must have, from the damage Tracey showed. She kept such a tight grip on herself and everything around her, as though that could prevent things from getting away from her. He wanted to tell her that it didn't matter. Things turned upside down and sideways in a moment, there was no way to hold on or recover.

"So he left, and you stayed at your home."

"For a while. It was familiar. Then I cut free and ran, before I just froze in place. It feels like an amputation sometimes—family, friends, places I knew—but it would have killed me to stay."

A vein was beating in her thumb. He felt it against the inside of his fingers. She let out a long breath that became a sigh, the unburdening of her heart, but there was more, he could feel something reserved. Private. He remembered reading a poem about women having no wildness in them, knew it was wrong then and wrong now. She was wild and shy, powerful but afraid that if she ever showed her softness, it would be savaged. Though the light was almost gone, he could see her face outlined against the window, and how her chin trembled.

He slid across the couch and put his arm around her shoulders. It was a brotherly hug, a moment of comfort that she accepted, and then he started to move back and his hand slid through her hair and stopped. He almost cried out at the rush of desire, the spike of blood in his heart. Her neck flexed, warm and solid, as she leaned back against his palm.

Her eyes were still wide but the wariness was overspread by a need that he recognized, for connection and touch. He bent and kissed her once, softly, and then returned. And returned.

The parlor enclosed them, shifts of fugitive light across the picture glasses and the darkness soft and enveloping. They lay side by side, his body fitting against hers. Her hips lifted when he moved.

Am I taking advantage of her? His nerve failed for an instant, he began to sit up, not wanting to cause her any more pain. But she touched his arm and he relaxed. *I have as much at risk as she does.*

He touched her breast through her dress, followed the contour, the softness and then the nipple. Her hips moved again, and her legs crossed his and he slid the one in the brace away. Blessed darkness. They lived in a cave of breath and touch, the lingering scent of oregano and honey on her hands, the green smell of her dress. No sight. No scars, nothing broken, nothing visible. He buried one hand in her hair and palmed the roundness of her skull beneath. He felt how her breast swelled from her ribs, the soft hollow beneath, the insistent rise of her mound.

She unbuckled his belt. He moved over her, wanting to pour himself into her, but when he lifted her dress he needed to touch the skin that had been under his hand, under the cotton, and he pulled the tie and released her breasts, kissed one and then the other, followed the recent path of his hand, counting her ribs with his tongue, the faint downy line of hair that led to her navel (omphalos, center of the world, the images bubbling up) and down to the wiry hair and the depths of her.

It was quick, the restraint of years shattered, and they were panting and sweaty against each other, the world settling back around them piece by piece. Like a snow globe, whirling and then the slow drift.

"Oh my God," he groaned.

"What?" She reached for his face and touched his ear, followed the line of his jaw to his lips.

"Are you—we didn't ..."

"I'm on the pill, if that's what you mean."

"That's what I mean."

The rest of the world came back, his leg aching from the pressure against it, the way his longer strands of hair had sprung free and lay pasted on his forehead. Reality, maybe, but his body still glowed, and hers trembled in short bursts.

"Are you okay?"

"Mmm-hmm. Aftershocks." And then she laughed, throaty and free of constraint.

He didn't want her to get up. She had to go to the bathroom, she said. He lay on his back for a moment, stretching, then got himself back together and sat on the edge of the couch.

Tracey came back, turning on a light on a side table, one of the ruffled-glass *Gone With the Wind* type. She was wearing a loose robe—a dashiki, he would have called it if one of his students wore it. Her face was pink and scrubbed; her hair was brushed. She sat down beside him on the couch. No words. The awkwardness of pulling back into their separate selves, back into the locked-away brain without body. No wonder chapters always ended with the sex scene and the movies cut away before this.

"Thank you," she said, and stunned him.

"No, you. I never expected."

"Me either. Well, you're staying, then."

Dave looked down. "I can bunk here."

"Crazy." She bumped his shoulder.

When she went upstairs, he paused at the foot of the steep staircase. Her robe shimmered under the harsh overhead light, wavering lines of blue and orange and purple moving into patterns that broke and formed again. Her bare legs were very white and her feet larger than they should be. Or maybe it was the perspective. His thoughts tumbled and he came close to going back to the couch and the security of being alone. She was almost to the top when he put his bad foot on the stairs and clumped after her.

A high white bed, white coverlet, white sheets. A tall lamp with a narrow shade. More non-ancestors on the wall, but on the chair was one of those old-fashioned bride dolls spreading its crocheted skirt. Tracey waited for him. She held out her arms and he moved into them, a kiss, not so intense. Goodnight kiss.

He took off his shirt and hung it on the chair back. His pants. He heard her lift off the robe in a slide of satin. He sat uneasily on the side of the bed and focused on the mechanics of his brace, trying to keep the process quiet. He stashed it under the chair, the bride doll staring at him with painted-on attention as he did. When he turned back, Tracey was naked.

"I usually sleep this way," she said, almost apologetically.

She had a farmer's tan, a V down her chest, white shoulders above a tan line that emphasized the firm muscles of her arms. But she was soft in her body, a little stomach, no more than classically allowed. *My God.*

She pulled back the covers and slid under. Dave leaned on the bed, trying to decide whether to shed his boxers, decided to keep them on. He got in—the bed was narrow, not even a double—she turned out the light and said goodnight and curled away from him.

Dave lay on his back, her shoulder pressed into his arm. The house was settling for the night, a hum from downstairs ending with a click, a low creak from a floorboard. He listened, heard two owls calling back and forth. The male was near the house, the female far away, her call lower and longer. Great horned owls, with ears and eyes like cats. The window was on her side, and he thought of her staring out, maybe following old memories across the sky with eyes that could see in the dark.

Chapter Fifteen

Tracey leaned into her spade, cut another slice into the slope. No plastic, just bottles and pottery and rusted metal. This dump seemed so remote from the farmhouses but there must have been other places around here. Maybe the kudzu took them, or the warm bug-rich nights that broke down even the brick chimneys. The old farms up in New England—she had walked with Carl, in the leaf season—old stone walls still outlined pastures, roads sunk deep below them, over time. But that area wasn't much older in settlement than this. Just poor soils and cold, up North; reclamation took centuries instead of decades.

She hadn't turned up anything on her blade for several feet, so she turned and began a new furrow across the area.

It helped to work. The sweat prickled along her hairline and under her breasts. Dave had driven away this morning, waving at her out the window. She waved back from the porch, smiling as widely. Then she became hollow and a little dizzy, as though she found that she'd been balancing on the edge of a tall building.

The memory of his hand on her breast and stomach made her thighs clench. He was gentle, respectful—but that was to be expected. That was who Dave was, at least on the outside. What was underneath, what right-angle turn to his personality?

Before Dave, before Carl, she'd dated a man who rode a motorcycle. She was never at ease. If she leaned into him, her hands gripped around his waist, then she couldn't see the road. If she leaned back and clutched the sides of the seat, she felt exposed and off balance, riding too high when they went into a turn. She had had to choose, ride blind, or sit straight and feel just how unstable two wheels were.

She lifted a shovelful of roots and blackened leaves, tossed them to the left—and there, movement. She let the shovel down slowly.

An old woman in a housedress and barn boots, carrying a stick and a milk jug, was coming down the hill from the Eccelston Road side. Tracey was close to the boundary, as she recalled it from walking the line in a steady rain, but she was rightfully on her land. And that was Artis's mother. Tracey had glimpsed her before, wispy white hair and broad face. The woman stopped at a thicket and reached in. Blackberries. Tracey watched her poke at the thicket with her stick, lift and push back the briers, wade in. It wouldn't take long for her to clear that patch, and there didn't seem to be others close by. With any luck she would turn away and Tracey would do the same.

But luck didn't hold. Maybe something caught the old woman's eye as it had hers, a little movement, a spark of light off a button. Artis's mother looked up from her bucket, shaded her eyes and then lifted her hand.

Oh, crap.

She backed out of the briers and came over, a brisk three-legged pace with the help of the walking stick.

"Good mornin'," she called out. "You having any luck over there?" She raised her milk jug and a layer of blackberries rolled from one side to the other.

"Hi. No, not much."

She stopped at the line, a straggle of ancient barbed wire sunk deep into trees where it had been nailed when they were saplings. "It rained on the blossoms and now it's come off hot and like to burn up the berries. I'd like me some blackberry jelly, could I get enough and the snakes leave me be." She banged the end of her stick twice on the ground.

For all the world, she's my grandmother. Tracey ached at the resemblance, from thin hair held back with black bobby pins to the whiskers sprouting from her chin. She wore an apron but no hat, and squinted against the sun.

"I guess you're not after berries."

"No—I'm—I look for things."

"History teacher, right? I guess that old stuff would have a pull on you. That's old Wayman's dump. Bachelor fella. You'll find precious little but tin cans and liquor bottles."

"Oh." So much for all the digging.

"He lived up yonder, little shack he built. Burned down in a lightning storm and took him with it. I was a fresh-married girl when that happened."

She looked where the woman pointed, but there was nothing to see but trees and underbrush, a little rise that maybe hid the foundation stones.

"He worked for my father, others around, when he felt like it. Couldn't rely on Wayman for anything needed, like finishing up a fence. He'd be half done and get a thirst and be gone. His family was solid folks, his brothers, but him—well, there's no accounting for men."

She cocked her head and looked hard at Tracey. The questions hung between them.

"A man isn't like a dog—you can't put a leash on him. He has to rely on his better nature." She made a sharp little nod. "Good luck, there."

CHAPTER SIXTEEN

Dave pulled his car under the deep shade of the white oak, a single great tree that stood an equal to the three-storied house with its wide verandahs. He glanced by habit at the massive horizontal limb that reached toward a corner room, the noiseless pathway he and Bert used from the time they could climb until—well, even college, remembering one predawn venture.

He had the novel he'd promised Sidney, prompted to unpack the books left this long in their moving boxes. Tuesday night he drove down to the Lowe's for bookshelves—the local home center didn't bother with knockdown furniture and such—and put them together with a screwdriver and some cursing. He was happy with the result, the worn Riverside Shakespeare in a place of honor, American poets on one shelf, Southern novelists on another.

The screen door still had fan-shaped fretwork in the corners, but the screen was freshly stretched and the door repainted its familiar white. Baskets of ferns hung from the ceiling, and the wicker chairs were the same though the cushions were now a bright tropical print. He used to slouch here, waiting on Bert or after one of their escapades, believing that the great oak could create a breeze in its deep green self when the air stood still and the whole world drooped. Cicadas buzzed and the sky burned, but as before, air moved across the porch.

He heard footsteps, scuffling, before Bert's mother came around the corner from the kitchen.

"Lord, Dave, but it's good to see you." She dried her hands on her apron and threw her arms around him. He returned the hug, not as firmly, feeling how soft her flesh was over small bones. "The rest are out back."

"Priming?"

"None too early. There's scald already, so they tell me." She wiped her hands again, staring down at her feet. They were swollen, the ankles round as columns and red, the slippers broken over on the sides. "I don't get out of the house much. Don't get out to help." She looked at him and smiled, making the effort to be bright. "But what brings you around?"

"I saw Sidney and he asked after a book I'd promised him back before school was out. I told him I had a copy but just had to find it." Dave held out the book, *Edisto*, covered in plastic, that he'd bought as the library purged its shelves of things that no longer circulated. Flannery O'Connor, Walker Percy. A shame.

"I'll put it up for him." She lifted one of the glass doors on the library case and set the book inside. Mostly the space was occupied with trophies, ribbons; what Bert hadn't won then Louise would have. A spelling bee dictionary, baseball, 4-H, track, Key Club, softball. There was the photo of the tennis team after the state finals, he and Bert leaning on their rackets, the Kodacolor starting to fade. It didn't look real. Each of them seemed scissored out of that mental picture, now, as though those were some other boys.

"Can I bring you some tea?"

"I'll stop out back," he said, hearing his mother's voice.

"I haven't seen you since your mother passed," Bert's mother said, gripping him by the forearm. She must had recognized the same turn of phrase, was reminded. "I miss her terrible, Dave. I know you do."

He couldn't tell her how his mother's death had come as a relief, her short illness more than he could bear on top of his own slow progress toward an incomplete recovery. He was ashamed to admit it. Not that he had ignored her, or done anything but what was right—still, he remembered sitting in the hard chair beside her hospital bed, studying her breathing. He didn't want to give her his breath. He hoarded his life, even as he despised it.

"We were a couple of old girls, there, for a while." She smiled.

"The bridge club, that was her outing, and mine. She always said we could have played professional, that's how good we were. Course it don't pay to be prideful."

He remembered something, some falling-out with others that came after the partners swept the tournament. It doesn't pay to set yourself up too high.

"Did you ever take up bridge?"

"No, not really." He felt ill at ease, as though she'd break out a deck of cards right there and test him. He could never beat his mother. She had a mind for math, wasted, they'd say now. Wasted on raising a single child. "I'll just go on out. It was nice to see you again."

"Go on with you, then." She cuffed him lightly on the shoulder, as though trying to knock away the formality between them. Dave ducked his head and went back out the front door. He wanted to run through the hall and burst through the back door and down the steps, but that was as likely as him calling Mrs. Bellamy by her first name, Melva. Neither was proper now.

A wash was hanging limply from the lines, propped up with forked poles. Nothing moving. The cicadas droned intermittently. The smell of the farm didn't so much reach him as envelop him—beef cattle in the fields, new hay in the barn, black muck drying along the edge of the pond where someone had used a Cat to dig out weeds and deepen the bed. This farm hadn't forgotten its roots—the Bellamys always had a little bit of everything going. Including tobacco, of course, and that's where he found them, in the field past the pond. An old woman wearing overalls and a T-shirt came scooting backward toward him through the rows, working on her knees. Her Indian braid slid back and forth as she pulled the yellowing lower leaves off the plants. She yelled after him, "Hey," as he passed, and he stopped, realizing it was Geneva Wade. When had her hair turned iron-colored?

"Hey, Geneva," he said back. The sharecropper's wife raised her head, her brow wrinkled as she looked up at him, but didn't stand.

"I thought that was you. 'Scuse me if I don't be getting up—hurt my back last winter and I still can't stoop."

"Sorry to hear that." He shaded his eyes—the rest of the crew was up at the top of the field, in a group.

"Yeah, Mr. Bellamy's up yonder." She pushed herself backward, the bundle of leaves thick under her arm.

"Want me to carry those on up?"

"You're a good boy, there. It's not the work, it's the getting up and down." She peeled the leaves from where they stuck under her arm, and he gathered the bundle and walked on, still shocked to find her creeping along the ground. She used to be tireless. She would throw fat hornworms at his head when he slacked.

He came across two young Latinos, then Sidney, who had that characteristic pallor under his freckled sunburn—the tobacco sap was getting to him—but he soldiered on, bending and plucking and stuffing the crinkled leaves under his left arm.

His grandfather raised a hand in greeting from the trailer where he was looping the leaves. "I'm helping out, show the boy," he explained, a little out of breath. "Good for him, to understand."

Dave nodded.

"His mother, she'd have him in a bubble if she could." The old man wiped the sweat from his forehead and pushed the straw hat back firmly. "Can't do that. Didn't do that with Bert. You neither."

Bert's father, the elder Sidney for whom the boy had been named, was short to the ground and stocky, almost gnomelike with the bend of years. Bert had taken after his mother's side, tall and lean.

"Sidney looks like his father," Dave observed.

"He does." The old man considered him for a long moment. "Has his grandmother's temperament though, thank God. Nothing fazes him."

"Bert took things to heart."

"He did."

Dave eased, not needing to avoid the subject. He'd been away teaching in Durham when it happened, but he knew most of it, how Bert's father had found his son down by the river with his shotgun between his legs, dead for hours. Bert had married halfway through college, a pert bright-haired girl from Florida. All the omens had been good. Mrs. Bellamy loved her and took her into the kitchen to pass on the secrets. Then the baby, right away. Then she just floated off. She flew home to see her parents one Thanksgiving and stayed, infatuated with some man. A frightening thing, how a touch, a look that goes on too long, could burn right through three, four lives. Like that soft white metal they kept in a jar in the chemistry lab, sodium or magnesium; if taken from the fluid that damped its nature, it would flame up in the air and couldn't be put out.

"Mr. Fordham?"

He shook his head, seeming to hear his father's name called, but seeing Bert peering in at the door.

Sidney shaded his eyes and looked up at him. "Mr. Fordham?"

"Sidney." Dave bent toward him, wishing he could hunker down and be face to face. "I brought that book I promised."

"All right!"

"It was at the bottom of the last box I looked into."

"Yessss!" Sidney started to pump his arm, and the leaves slid—he might have dumped them right there, but his grandfather's glance was enough. The others continued at their pump-jack labor, standing and stooping, and Sidney didn't have leave to go.

"It'll be there. In the library case."

Sidney nodded. "I guess."

Dave put a hand on his shoulder. "You enjoy it. Let me know if you want another recommendation." The boy didn't look up, but the edges of his mouth worked toward a grin. The white showed too plain when he did—the nicotine seeping through his skin. It was hard being a scrawny kid in the fields. Dave had thrown up for two days, his first year, but his father said it would pass and he'd get used to it. And he had. There was a kind of honor in sticking it out.

"He's got the sick," the old man said, suddenly close behind them.

"Yeah."

"You and Bert both got through it."

"Yeah."

Sidney hoisted his leaves to the trailer and headed up field. He didn't ask for grace, didn't see how his grandfather watched after him. "We're stopping right soon—lunchtime. I won't have him back out in the afternoon sun."

"That's probably best." The boy tended toward his mother's coloring.

"I know I seem to be living in the past, Dave." He bent and

broke off a leaf, tucked it under his arm, almost automatically. "The smart folks hire this done. I do, too, mostly. I just hate to see all of it forgotten. What I learned from my dad, him from his dad." The memory of Bert waited in the silence.

"Remember that time?" The old man laughed. Dave didn't have to say a word. "That time Bert got himself stuck in the curing barn?"

"Yeah." Dave still felt the pang. He was in on the prank, wild with the excitement of doing it, crazy with fear to tell.

"We were like never to find him. Night come on, no Bert. He said he yelled and hammered and carried on till he passed out."

"I remember."

"Good thing someone thought to check the barn, or he like to died in there."

Dave had whispered to Bert's mother, and she had told them to look there. She never told a soul, that he knew of. Now he wondered if Bert's father knew, maybe had known. They went back out in the evening, past the livestock barn and the cribs to the idle curing barn, set back near the fields. The door was shut and the pin had seemed to work partway down in the latch—a freak accident. Thick heat rolled out of the airless space like smoke, and Bert lay motionless on the floor. The men had raised him up and carried him into the cool, ghost-white and staggering, Lazarus raised to die again.

"You were all wild, wouldn't put a thing past any of you. Now I worry about that one, what he'll do."

The boy was working his way back, pulling the leaves with an exaggerated motion. Testing his muscles and how they slid over the bones. Dave had the same physical memory, how he marveled at the working of ligament and tendon, arms extended and knees strained in tennis, the skin-deep hurt of brush burns and the deeper bruises of an errant baseball. He had more confidence then in his body than his brain—but cocky about both. Here in this field the memories of Bert were more physical, not thin nostalgia but a loss of a genuine part of himself—the pal, the partner who knew where to juke, when to shift his weight. Good memories, though the shadows seemed too long and deep where they met his friend's recalled shape—a ball game with the sun almost gone, the field flaming green. The shroud flung out from Bert's floating form, the catch itself lost in shadow.

He had lost his grip, that much Dave knew of himself. The broken bones and severed nerves had healed as well as they ever would, but the other part—what could he offer someone? His crippled foot was the least of what had been damaged in that Baltimore gutter. He had been trying not to think about Tracey—the ache he had put aside, her reserve that fell away before unashamed desire and afterward returned. He couldn't help but see himself through her eyes. His hunched and club-footed self. But a deep hope, maybe as wild as that boy had been, that she saw something else in him, something that was starting to come clear of the thick undergrowth. When they were together, his problems seemed to disappear for long moments.

"*Serpiente! Serpiente!*"

One of the kids shouted and danced back, shedding tobacco as he did. Sidney came flying up the row and out of the field.

"Copperhead?" the old man asked, his voice shaky.

No one was working. The grandfather was as afraid as any of them—and Bert had been terrified of snakes—so that, too, was being passed down.

Dave found a hoe and went quietly to where the first boy had panicked. He listened for the movement of snake against soil, watched for the shiver in a plant where there wasn't a breath of wind. Nothing. He moved forward, rustling the hoe ahead of him. Out of the corner of his eye he saw a rust-brown pattern shift, resolve, blend back into the soil. He swung the hoe around and pinned the snake behind its head. It didn't thrash, just seemed to wait for the sharp edge of the hoe to come down again. He rolled the blade away from the snake, twisted his wrist and brought it back underneath and lifted it.

"Corn snake," he said.

"*Serpiente!*"

"No," he said, balancing the three-foot snake on the hoe. "Muy bueno. Muerte raton."

He'd mangled the Spanish but thought they got the idea.

Both Sidneys had come back, though not too close. He carried the snake, limp as a dead thing, to the far side of the field and flung it toward the woods. It fell into weeds and the movement showed it headed for the shade.

"You can tell from the pattern," he told them. "And the head—it didn't have the big flat head and skinny neck."

"I'm not planning on getting that close," the old man said.

"You just have to respect them," Dave said, more to the boy. He'd been taught snake-sense. "Most of them do a lot of good, kill vermin."

"I recollect your grandfather was that way. He said as long as he could see what it was, he was okay with sharing the field. I can't bear to look at the things to tell what it is."

Dave smiled. He felt the flush of things moving right for the first time in a long time. It was like learning to return serve—he could feel as he set down the hoe that some things learned weren't lost.

"We moved a building, one time, and broke up a snake den," the elder Sidney began. "Nobody home, summertime. Rattlesnakes keep dens for the winter. If you get rid of the dens, you get rid of the snakes—they'll die before they go somewhere else. But that den, we pulled a shed skin out of it over seven foot long. Great huge rattle on it."

One snake story led to another. Dave remembered telling Tracey, after a long discussion in the lounge, that every Southerner carried a whole book of snake stories around in his head.

The dinner bell rang by the kitchen door, and they all turned for the house carrying the late excitement with them. Dave was thinking about house foundations and digging, about Tracey in her middens, barely listening when he heard the old man say he was going out of tobacco.

"You're not."

"Yep." He nodded emphatically. "This is our last priming."

"What about the farm?"

"Just because I don't plant tobacco don't mean I don't farm."

Dave winced inwardly, waiting for his old friend's father to say he was going into emus, or llamas, or one of the other schemes that floated through the Old Belt as farmers tried to hang on.

"That's why I wanted Sidney to see. So he knew more about it than out of a book. But I know we gotta change. Heck, back in the old days they raised cotton here. We don't do that now. I'm putting one section into herbs for the city folk. Rosemary and such."

"That's a good idea." Dave was relieved.

"And meat goats. The Mexicans like goat, and down in the city they got a lot of folks from the Holy Land. They ain't nothing to raising a goat on poor ground."

Dave went up the back steps, and Mrs. Bellamy was holding a platter of tomatoes. The old man hung his hat on the same hook as always. Dave took the platter from her hands and carried it to the table, set it in front of Sidney and set himself down across from him, waiting with a clear heart for prayer to be said.

CHAPTER SEVENTEEN

Other than the heat, there wasn't much to distinguish the Shawton Summer Celebration from the Persimmon Pickin' that highlighted the fall calendar. People ambled up the main street toward the soldier at picket on his plinth, idling past booths that sold crafts and slices of pecan pie. Some were the same vendors from the weekly farmers' market, in the same location. Kids played in loose groups that split and reformed as parents moved and talked, moved on. A bluegrass band faded in and out under the huffing of a generator that powered the Moon Walk, and somewhere a dog barked and barked.

The difference, Tracey knew, was only in herself.

Last summer, spent making the house habitable, was a summer spent alone. If others like her—like her as she had been—moved through the county's events, then she didn't see them or have the time to, moving purposefully from craft table to lemonade stand, determined to have fun.

As Dave stopped to speak with someone she didn't know, Tracey touched his arm and moved ahead to talk with Gloria, presiding alone over the eggs and honey.

"Where's Harley?"

"Oh, he's tired this morning."

Was his health failing? His heart?

"He shoveled out the chicken houses yesterday and built up the compost—he said he'd stay home and see to the cooking today."

So much for old age.

Dave caught up and whispered an apology.

"Gloria, this is Dave," she said, and stopped—Gloria didn't seem to expect more, just stuck out her hand and smiled. Tracey didn't know quite what to say, friend being too casual, lover far too intimate, boyfriend too childish. Even if she could have defined their relationship, she wasn't sure she wanted to put a name to it.

"Nice to meet you, in the flesh."

He blushed, which Tracey had come to learn he did easily.

"You make some good honey."

"Not me. Thank the bees. And the year. Here, try this."

She handed him a honey straw, which he broke open and drained onto his tongue.

"Locust blossom," she said.

"This was the year for it, wasn't it? The bloom rained out of the trees near the school."

"Tons of nectar. I was hauling full supers out and slamming empties in like piecework. Here." She pressed a honey bear into Dave's hand.

"We'll enjoy it," Dave said, glancing to Tracey for confirmation, and she almost put her hand against the fullness in her chest.

Dave asked how much it was, and Gloria waved him away. "Come out again," she said to Tracey, and then tilted her head back toward Dave. "And bring him too, okay?"

Dave tucked the plastic bear into a cargo pocket on his pants. Tracey had thought his outfit looked a little goofy, a loose cotton shirt in madras and the olive-drab slacks, but she had to admit it was practical. She held onto her purse and a bag with a pair of potholders and wished she could tuck them away.

They worked their way through the festival. Dave knew almost everyone, but whether it was his own reticence or the fact that she was with him, the encounters were mostly nods, a word here or there. Ray Koch teetered on his heels at a table offering "Free Water" and "Living Water," the latter being red-covered booklets of the Gospels. Students avoided him, and them—it must be bad luck to run into a teacher out of season.

In such a crowd, Tracey couldn't help but wonder who had left those violent calls on her answering machine, what kind of people hid behind bland faces she didn't recognize.

In front of the courthouse, long tables had been set up for the contests—right now, parents whooped as kids chewed their way through slabs of watermelon. Juice slicked their faces and soaked the newsprint that covered the tables. One big kid already had piled six rinds by his plate and was reaching for a seventh when an air horn bleated.

"Time!" Mike Keener stepped forward, wearing a big grin and an oversized "Judge" ribbon pinned to a SAUL COUNTY CITIZEN golf shirt. A black camera hung around his neck. "Looks like we've got a winner. Zeke Soles!"

The big kid stood up and made a little embarrassed bow. His mother was gesturing at him and he took a towel and wiped off his face and neck.

"Zeke, want to tell us what school you go to?"

"Wysock Memorial High School," he said, and when a few boos came from the back, raised his fist. "Go Wolverines!"

"Zeke's a lineman on the JV team—I bet Coach Tipton can't wait to get you into the varsity. Here's your prize, courtesy of the Saul County Chamber of Commerce and the *Citizen*—two movie passes and a family chicken basket from the Country Market." Mike stepped back and took pictures as the Chamber president pinned a blue ribbon on the boy's sopping shirt and handed him the envelope.

Mike had seen them at the edge of the crowd and waved, so Tracey felt compelled to say hi. As the watermelon was cleared away to make room for the next contest (hot dog eating), he came over and presented each of them with a *Citizen* pen.

"Promotions," he said, with a wry smile that was undercut by the obvious joy with which he boosted his paper. He'd become the editor-in-chief last week, an occasion that demanded two columns on the front page.

"Congratulations," Tracey said. "How do you like being editor?"

"I get to sit at the head table at the county dinners." He reached between them to dispense a fistful of pens. "Remember the *Citizen*! But I still write a good bit."

"Do you think you'll go to twice a week?" Dave asked. "I remember when the *Citizen* came on Tuesdays and Fridays."

"Not soon, anyway. The economy just isn't there. And equipment, all that. Kinda like that house of yours—you have to rip one thing out before you can add something new." He bumped his knuckles against Tracey's shoulder, which surprised her—and made Dave move a step closer.

"Yes," she said.

Mike seemed to realize his misstep. "I couldn't get her to answer the phone, so I went out to her house to get a quote."

"I know," Dave said.

Mike said he was needed at the judge's table, and his attention switched just that quickly—a distracted word of goodbye and he was off to the next thing.

It was nearly eight. Tracey said she was hungry and they headed back through the crowd. They ordered two sausage sandwiches and Cokes and found a bench under a scrawny pair of crape myrtles. Dave was quiet, worrying at the rough edge, the little slippage of doubt. She didn't try to draw him out, but as she finished her sandwich she reached over and took his hand and squeezed. It was enough. His eyes accepted that reassurance.

The festival was shifting into the evening program, music and the wait for darkness and the fireworks. A gospel quartet harmonized despite an unsteady baritone. They walked back on the other side of the street, but Dave wasn't interested in the booths any more.

"Ready to go?"

Tracey hadn't expected that. She had told him how much she loved fireworks, how Independence Day wasn't complete until the last shell faded.

"I guess." She hadn't thought that Mike's pushiness had bothered him so. At least there had been no sign of Artis, though she'd done a double-take once at a red pickup.

Dave swung the car out of the lot and onto Tennon Avenue, but at the light turned left.

"It's a nice night for a ride, isn't it?"

"Sure."

The sky darkened as they headed into the country. The evening star showed, clear white, above the trees. Tracey had driven all over the county at one time or another, but this wasn't a road she had revisited. It wound toward no particular destination—maybe a village had been there once, in that far corner of the county, but no longer. Dave put on his signal, though there wasn't a car in sight, and went up a narrow road that climbed one of the rounded hills. She didn't feel uneasy, not with Dave, though she considered how well she really knew him, and then put that doubt away.

The road topped out beside a white church and a little graveyard. Woods turned into pastures and back to woods as the land sloped down to a river, gleaming in the last light. It was the Dorset, she was pretty sure, though the Humber curved down through the county here. Settlers had put the names of placid English rivers to these in Carolina, though they ran red in flood and low in summer.

"Watch."

She watched the stars, identifying constellations. She watched the headlights on the road. She watched the sunset fade to the last strip of purple.

The crickets and cicadas sawed away. A mockingbird sang like a cardinal, and then a song sparrow, and then something she didn't know, three phrases each time.

A distant whump, and a star shell opened, white and then red.

Tracey took his hand, and they watched the flowering of the sky.

"Have you always come up here to watch?"

"For some while." Dave let go of her hand and put both of his on the steering wheel, leaned forward as though to see better. "When I was a kid we used to walk over to the ball field and watch the firemen set them off. They wouldn't run us off as long as we stayed out of the bleachers." Nothing more, though she could feel that he had more to say.

He lifted his chin to indicate the river below.

"That's the bridge."

She looked at the road, how it crossed the river on a plain concrete span.

"Dad had just crossed the bridge when the deer came out of the woods. A big buck, but they're sure he never saw it because of the trees along the fence. Jumped right into his car, right through the windshield."

"Is that what happened?"

"It killed him. Just a freak thing. He'd run over to a dealer in Blossom County and was on his way back. Routine."

Tracey looked straight out at the fireworks. What to say. I'm sorry? How can you be sorry about something that happened years ago, decades? Dave had always seemed to dismiss his father, repeating the stories about his philandering, his emotional distance. But to have died like that. Her own father was an aching memory, set in relief by her mother's bitterness that kept them apart except when she went to the farm, his mother's home, and those days were always so precious. By the time she could make her own choices, he'd moved on to a new wife and a second family.

"I always thought if we'd had more time," Dave said, even lower. "Maybe. I guess that's what everyone thinks. That it would have been different."

The echo of Carl's voice: "I wish it could have been different."

Memories of their marriage opened one into another, like the sprays of light opening and fading to be overcome by the next. The apartment on West High Street, honeymoon, first anniversary, buying a bed, the U-Haul broken down and spraying steam on the side of 70 East, shoveling snow, grading papers together. More time. The Fourth of July before the silences widened into a split, they went to Conneaut Lake Park. Rode the Wild Mouse. Watched the fireworks reflected in the lake. How they bickered in the car, hot and tired, the traffic jam, the greasy food roiling in her stomach.

"It doesn't matter."

Dave jerked, maybe lost in his own memories.

"More time. If we had it, we wouldn't know that we did. There's only the present. The rest of it is just hopes or memories."

"And regrets. You're right, you Buddhist—be here now, the rest is illusion." He gave her that all-or-nothing smile, and she leaned into it as if falling onto a deep, comforting pillow.

They held each other as the final fusillade went off, distant mortars like the sound of someone banging on a basement door. The sky was filled with umbrellas of fire, daisies, bursts, whirling dots. When it was dark again, they drove home, and when they got out of the car Garland slid his rough back against her leg.

CHAPTER EIGHTEEN

The wood groaned, then splintered, one piece skittering across the floor.

Tracey stumbled, her weight all forward against the pry bar, put out a hand and recovered. The old wood should crack like balsa, or so you'd think, but this was tough stuff, seasoned pine that wasn't ready to let go.

She put the teeth of the bar under the chair rail and leaned on the other end. The next section broke free to the joint. Onto the scrap pile. She'd like to be able to pry a single forgiving word out of Orenna Sipe's mouth. It has been weeks since she'd seen her, months since the attack, but this morning in town it was the same. She came around a display at the dollar store and Orenna was digging through a bin of towels. Not a word. She just stared, the same hostility, but Tracey wasn't caught flat-footed this time. She nodded, smiled a little—the opening, if Orenna wanted—instead, Lakesha's mother had bundled up her things and walked quickly toward the checkout. You'd think she had killed the child instead of trying to help.

Coal dust filtered out from the wall, with a little sound like wind on sand, and when the dust had settled that thin crackling sound continued inside the wall. Crumbling bits of wood escaped at the bottom of the bead board. She'd take all this off today.

Hot already, and she was sweating—that was good. Right. It helped to sweat and feel her muscles. She'd learned that from her father when she was just little. Daddy's girl, helping him out around the house in her overalls and little Converse sneakers. She'd learned from him that when you got angry, it was best to find some chore and work it out. She hadn't understood then what it was he was angry about. He never talked about anything, but he took great satisfaction out of tearing things down and building them back.

This wall, covered a third of the way up with heavily painted wainscoting and topped with a too-thick chair rail, hadn't been original to the kitchen. The trim was added sometime, the '40s or '50s, maybe to make a "breakfast nook" or some such idea. It was one of the jobs she'd reserved for herself—contractors had taken enough of her cash replacing the water heater, patching the roof, and installing a furnace in the damp, clay-walled basement to replace gas heaters stuck in front of defunct fireplaces.

She started to pry on the last section of molding, but the bead board gave alarmingly when she leaned on it. She reset the bar in a firmer location and tried again. The nails (spikes, not finishing nails) bent and popped free.

Tracey realized long after her father was gone that his constant renovations had been his way of keeping himself in that house. He was needed. He was always hammering and painting. Her mother took it all in with tight smiles, but at night they would argue behind the closed bedroom door. Her father couldn't keep himself in the family, no matter how hard he worked at keeping up the place. When her mother filed the papers, he had moved out and left his tools behind. It was a constant project, maintaining a marriage, any relationship. Like with Dave—what was she building on? She knew the outlines of his life, what had been taken away, but there were always hidden things. Down in the foundation. What someone else had made strong or weakened. And what she knew of her own heart, did he understand even a little?

She took the scrap out and around back to the burning place. Easier to burn it than cart it, as generations had done here.

The paneling would come off in big sections. Then she could drywall and spackle, then wallpaper. Twining ivy, an old-fashioned pattern that fit this kitchen and wouldn't be hard to match.

Dave was a good man. No doubt of that. At least, she didn't doubt, though he did. It was the one thing that pushed her away, his lack of confidence. He'd gone into his shell after being hurt and never really come back out. That wasn't her way—she moved, she made things happen. God knows. That mess with Artis, all her doing. She didn't understand these Southern men, still stuck on the plantation with Scarlett. Just the thought of him churned things up. What was Artis capable of? She couldn't believe he would do, could do, anything more than he'd already done. He hadn't exactly stalked her, though she saw his truck and him more than usual. She couldn't prove that he or Jim had done anything, scratched her car or set nails under her tires, tossed a dead raccoon onto her porch. The phone calls had stopped, since no one knew her number. It wasn't long now until the trial. Sometimes at night she wavered, decided she would not testify, but by morning she was strong again. Soon it would all be over with.

She retied the scarf over her hair and put on a paper mask. This was going to be dusty, no doubt.

The first panel was stubborn, the long nails holding as she pulled and pried. When it was off, she found about what she had expected— uninsulated space between raw studs, diagonal board sheathing of the outside wall, wiring covered with braided fabric, coal dust. And a strange, dank smell. The next panel came more easily, and the smell got stronger. She wondered what had crawled into the walls and died. The attic had been a mausoleum of mummified birds, baby squirrels, paper wasp nests crumbling with age. A little spur of excitement—maybe a jar full of old coins had been hidden—came and left quickly. People didn't really do that, and she wasn't the lucky sort to find a stash if there was one. Tracey jabbed the bar under the next panel and gave a strong push. The nails creaked free. Up around the top, then the far corner—the whole panel popped loose, and what spilled out wasn't gold or jewels, but it was the source of the smell.

Termites poured out of the channeled wood like salt from a bag. Like maggots from a corpse. The studs were holed through, like rotten curtains, and the outside wall was eaten to the asbestos cement shingles.

Tracey backed away, tore off the mask so she could breathe, but the smell was so thick, acid and damp, that she held it back to her nose.

The termites wriggled on the floor, turning away from the light. Like maggots. Soft white bodies. Some had dark, ugly pincers, and they ran around the edges of the mass waving their weapons.

Infested. She shuddered at the sight of them, horrible, the hidden rot. Her house consumed from within. But there were no signs, no sounds, no leavings, no dirt. What she knew about termites came from the funny billboards along the highway. Funny as a crutch, the images of tilting houses and marching armies of white termites.

She stood for a while, watching the creatures spill out of the collapsed tunnels. She didn't want to think about the ceilings overhead and the walls, the soft sound she hadn't recognized, the creaking that had been the innocent sound of an old house but now seemed like the cry of the whole thing falling in from termites.

Finally the sight of them creeping back toward the dark inside the walls forced her to move.

There was no one to call. Dave was in Raleigh getting his CEUs. No exterminator would come out on a Sunday. This was her business, hers to deal with. She got a broom and a flat shovel, and she swept the creatures into a pile and shoveled them into a trash bag. When one fell onto her hand she dropped the bag, repulsed by the cool writhing body.

She had ant spray under the sink. They were ants, she remembered, nightmare ants. Industrious in a perverted way, instead of building and hoarding they turned the solid world into air, into their own wormy bodies, into more termites forever. She sprayed into the cavity. And when she saw pincers coming through the plastic bag, she sprayed the mass and tied it up, took it out to the burn-pile. She ran for the can of charcoal fluid, sprayed it thickly everywhere and threw lit matches. The fluid breathed fire and the plastic bag melted. Termites twisted. She threw on the paper mask and watched the flames get high and hot.

Tracey sat down on the front steps. The sun was clean, baking away the residue that seemed to stick to her. The old-fashioned flowers she had planted bent this way and that, heavy-headed cleome, zinnias, cosmos. Morning glories tangled through them, and the awkward green plants called summer poinsettia.

I had to be out of my mind. This house, this whole thing.

Tracey thought about the jobs she might have gotten, in a city, where she could have lived in a clean anonymous apartment. Running away from Pennsylvania had been a mistake, thinking that she could really start over somewhere this different, that she could walk into someone else's history and find a refuge. What did she get? A thankless job, a death at her doorstep, hostility, violence, and now the place she lived ready to come down around her ears.

God, I could just bawl.

She pulled a flower off the cosmos and tossed it aside, broke off a leaf and began to tear it to pieces. Milky latex ran out—poinsettia, even if all it showed was a little orange spot on the leaves—the white sap only reminded her of the gnawing things inside the walls. She feared it all, the termites, the people, the dogs, the tangle around Artis of attraction and revulsion, Dave's memories insinuated into hers until she could feel the cold and the blows and the bones breaking. Her eyes were sandy and her throat tight. You were just supposed to let it out. That's what they said. She remembered her father trimming a huge hedge, the only sound his clippers closing and opening, the branches sliding to the ground.

Tracey pulled a clump of grass from the crack between the porch and the flower bed. Heavy hayfield grass, dark green, the stems thick. Her grandmother had showed her how to whistle using coarse grass. She hadn't been able to whistle, pursing her lips and blowing until her face hurt. "Here," her grandmother said, "is a trick with a hole in it." She pulled a piece of grass and layered it between her thumbs. "Like doing this is the church, this is the steeple. Put the grass between the doors. Then blow into that crack." Her grandmother made a piercing whistle between her own thumbs. She gave Tracey that same blade of grass, set it between her thumbs and folded her fingers. She saw the veins under the papery skin and realized that her grandmother was old. Old.

Her Grandma Flora had always seemed the same. She wore green barn boots outside and a flowered dress and a straw hat in the summer to keep off the sun. "I burn that easy—just like you will. Red hair." Tracey escaped the tension at home by staying with her grandmother through the summers, helping out after Grandpa was gone. She was in ninth grade when her grandmother started to sit down more, catch her breath, ask Tracey to run upstairs or down to the mailbox. She was happy to be her grandma's feet.

The next summer, Tracey saw pill bottles lined up over the sink. Her grandma said little about the doctor visits. Tracey didn't understand until she heard her mother talking on the phone. "She's eaten up with cancer," she said. "Just eaten up inside."

They all wanted Tracey there more, to do the laundry and the lawn mowing. Her grandmother, though, wanted something else. Wanted to talk about the past, her own girlhood. Tracey avoided the family stories—there was something to do outside. She shoveled and cut brush, took on chores the neighbor men would have done. It kept her from facing the sagging skin and sunken eyes and the way her grandmother was emptying out her past.

Her grandmother had eaten a good meal that night, tuna casserole and tomatoes from the garden, canned peaches from last summer. Tracey had carried it on a tray to her hospital bed and then eaten by herself at the table. Her grandmother's mouth was sore from the treatments and her dentures didn't fit, so she smashed food on her plate and slurped the mess past her bleeding gums.

Tracey had cleaned up the kitchen and was watching TV when she heard the crash.

She ran to the small bedroom beside the kitchen. She saw the white-gowned figure on the floor beside the broken lamp. She hit the switch and the harsh overhead light and the smell came at the same time, so that she cringed back from the door.

"Tracey." Her grandmother's hand reached up, trembling; it seemed like the light poured through it. A pool spread past her legs, dark and gummy, blood, feces. Her insides coming out. The treatments had eaten her away until the last barrier was crossed and she was coming apart on the floor.

She made the two steps; it seemed like it took a long time. Her grandmother clutched the leg of her jeans until she could sit up and lean against the bed. Tracey could reach the black telephone on the bedside table and she called the number for the volunteer fire department inked and re-inked on the sticker.

Tracey thought she could pick her up and get her back on the bed, but her grandmother wouldn't allow it. Instead, Tracey hunkered down beside her and held onto her hand, for a long time, while a crew gathered and ran the ambulance out from town. The siren rose and fell in the distance, getting louder, until the red lights spun across the room. Tracey stood aside as the garage man and the woman who ran the rest home brought in a stretcher and took her grandmother away.

When her grandmother was in the hospital, Tracey didn't visit. When she died, she wouldn't go sit by the body or attend the funeral. She stayed in her room, watching TV, listening to her divorced mother and father arguing about her though they wouldn't speak two words otherwise. She had turned away, and her grandmother had died without seeing her again, the granddaughter she said was dearer to her than her own daughter. Tracey didn't know what that meant, until Carl left and would not come back, and she lay alone at night and longed for his touch just one more time.

A tear hit the step. Then another.

Oh, sweet Jesus.

Tracey knew what she was. If you kept moving, the pain couldn't catch up. If you kept moving, you could keep control, could avoid breaking down and letting the wind blow through your bones.

She wasn't there for her grandmother, though she'd tried to bottle that up, remembering the summers when she was there, was her grandmother's child. At the end, she abandoned her. It was fear, yes, it was, but not what people thought. It was like Lakesha. She wasn't afraid of death, of her grandmother's, maybe even of her own. It was the child, it was the thought of that torn child asking for her help. Because that kind of pain wasn't bearable. It would smash through her control and break her apart.

That was happening now. She'd been gnawed apart. Nothing would hold together.

CHAPTER NINETEEN

Lester was working the crowd.

Pickups and cars were still coming in, but most of the farm families were already gathered under the trees at the north edge of the gravel lot. Coolers were set up on tailgates and blankets spread on the grass for the babies. Lester strolled among them in his Carolina-blue seersucker jacket, smiling, passing out business cards. He seemed confident, walking lightly despite his girth. His jowly face was pink and friendly.

"Who's he?"

"A wheeler-dealer," Dave told her, low enough. "Lester Cordwainer. He buys up land."

There was more he could have said, but didn't. Tracey was up in arms about the rows of manufactured housing that cordoned the fields close by where her friend the honey woman lived. That was Lester's first project, built on the land he inherited from his grandparents. Most developers didn't dirty their own backyards.

"Come on. I want you to look around before things get started."

The auctions had started the end of July down in the southeastern part of the state. Whiteville, Fair Bluff. Price reports were read on the radio every morning as the auctions opened in their turn across the Old Belt. It was time for Saul County's, here at Shawton and in Taberville and over at the lone warehouse in what had been the village of Redstick.

You have to see this, he had told Tracey. This may be the last time there'll be a tobacco auction.

Leaf Pride II Warehouse was painted in tall serif letters on the side of the metal building, put up four years ago to replace a crumbling brick structure. Huge doors were pushed back on both sides to let the air through. As soon as they got out of the car the thick sweet smell of cured bright-leaf flowed across them.

Dave loved the life cycle of tobacco, the culture that surrounded it, even if the plant made him sick and its final product was so devastating. People from outside tobacco country didn't understand that affection for the crop. They were used to wheat or corn, seeded and harvested, but not tended with that kind of intimacy. Tobacco was hand-raised from start to finish, from seeds planted in the greenhouse to the tender young plants set into the furrows from the back of a tractor, from weeding and priming and topping to pulling and racking and curing. All by hand. Even the enemies of tobacco seemed personal, farmers complaining bitterly of blue mold as though it had singled out their fields. It was a good part of life, to see the fields flourish in the summer sun, and then to follow tractors and wagons down the two-lane roads with green leaf gathered in the old way across the sticks, on its way to propane-driven curing barns while old log barns decayed picturesquely under morning glory and kudzu. Finally, the cured leaf tied up in burlaps like giant hobo bindles and carried off to warehouses and auction.

He'd told Tracey all this, in bits and pieces, and she had caught a bit of the nostalgia—her historian's interest piqued by anything that was passing away.

The owner was standing outside the plywood office built at one end of the warehouse. He paced back and forth, greeting most of the latecomers with a strong handshake and a slap on the shoulder. Dave could almost feel what he was feeling, see it in the space of concrete bare of tobacco, in the light turnout of farmers. He could tally who was missing, the people his parents' age who had farmed tobacco and quit. There were some farmers his own age, but fewer, the generations falling off. They had kids in school, Harrises and Stringers and Demornays. Maybe a tithe of them would still be raising leaf in a few years, and it would go straight to the buyers without this social event, outdated as a cake walk.

"There's Dewayne," Tracey said, and turned him to see one of the few black families here. The student hunched his shoulders to get down closer to the level of his wiry father and mother—that size, and the Cs he managed at the alternative school, had him back on the Dragons' line this fall.

"Look there." Dave pointed at the whiteboards on the wall beside the office. Printed in blue and red letters: LAST WEEK OLD BELT REPORTS. New leaf 171-182. Lugs 156-166. Primings 139-145.

"The first auctions clear out the poor stuff," he explained. "Carryover that didn't sell last season—the cooperative will mostly take that, at a guaranteed minimum price. And the low-quality stuff."

"Primings—the first leaves they pick," Tracey said.

"Pull."

"Pull." She made an exasperated face.

"Sorry."

"No, I want to know the right words. It's just so...specific."

It's the language of a whole world, he almost said. A dying language. He was one of the ones who would remember words layered with the memories. Coming to the original Leaf Pride, he had been among a pack of kids running around while the auctioneer chanted his way along the piles, their fathers watching with steady concern the hand signals of buyers from American, Philip Morris, Dimon. They vibrated with the promise of ice cream after the auction and then a trip to Raleigh. Like always, folks would be flush with auction money—once the warehouse and the auctioneer and the feed store and the gas company were paid, the families would buy school clothes and long-delayed necessities. The less able or less lucky would be at the pawn shop getting guns and engagement rings out of hock.

He scanned the crowd for familiar faces, still, she spotted Artis before he did, nudging him to look across the warehouse and see him standing with one heel cocked against the wall. Jim stood beside him, head down. Dave had the feeling Artis had been watching them for a while, the steady gaze, the way he lifted his hand in a slightly mocking salute. He nodded back. Jim kicked his oversized Nikes against the floor.

"I see he's enjoying his freedom," she said.

Tracey appeared casual about it, but Dave couldn't pretend to be. Artis showed up too often, even for a place this small; his comments were reported around town and if Dave heard them, she surely did as well. He worried that she was keeping herself and the whole situation too tightly under wraps. The other day she'd rambled on about the termites she'd found while he was at in-service training, and the tension in her voice made him wonder if that's all there was to it, just a few termites let loose from the walls of an old house.

He took Tracey's hand and she squeezed his in return. They strolled toward the far end of the warehouse. She had adapted her stride to his, so easily that sometimes he forgot how she used to move—like someone in a hurry who didn't want to appear that way, covering ground. Now she walked with formal deliberation and her grace raised him up. They crossed in front of the open doors and in the breeze her hair streamed across his face like sparks. "Sorry," she said, pulling it back and winding it into a loose coil that would break free at the next breeze. He didn't say a thing, just brought her a little closer and blessed his luck.

What he couldn't tell her, with the dread she bore of the teachers and students and parents, the memories, and the trial itself, was how he was looking forward to school this year. He hadn't put in a bid for transfer, as he had in each of the past years. Arbogast asked him, had he forgotten, "Although I would not want to lose you, Mr. Fordham." And he had made light of it, that there was little difference any more between the regular schools and A.O. Miller. The fact was he didn't want to change a thing. Not his tired room, the desk with the sticking drawers, the marred door, the drafty windows. Not the joy he felt turning into the potholed drive a week ago, checking his mail cubby, preparing for another full load of students just like the ones the year before and the year before. Because the best mornings now found him sitting on Tracey's front porch, sipping coffee and watching the big sulfur butterflies of late summer drift from flower to flower.

Not that he felt sure of himself. Tracey had an unsettling way of looking at him sometimes, as though she moved him around in her thoughts and maybe held him up against something or someone past. Sometimes he felt like Garland must. The black-and-white cat had made a decision to move into the human sphere, sitting on the porch as they read or talked, seemingly asleep but ready to jump if Dave tried to pet him. Tracey was allowed to stroke his bony back, and he eased under her touch but never rolled to show his stomach nor allowed his ragged ears to be scratched. Things were good so far, so far as he allowed.

They had rotated back with the crowd, swirling into place as the auctioneer tested his wireless microphone and the speakers crackled and hummed.

"What's with the parade?" she asked.

The auction crew was gathering at the first row, the auctioneer in his mustard-yellow shirt, the representatives of the co-op and the USDA and the buyers. It was a sizable group that trailed the auctioneer as he set off at a fair walk.

"You see the papers—that's the grade set by the government inspector." Each pile of tobacco was opened, the burlap peeled back so the cured leaves showed and on each one, a white slip. Each pile was auctioned separately, going down to the hand signals flickering from the brokers. "The women have ribbons for each company— they throw them down on the pile to mark the buyer. And the clerks write the price and grade and grower and toss a copy on the pile."

"Seems labor-intensive."

"Yeah, but it works."

The auctioneer's chant was subdued. He wasn't flashy like some Dave remembered, but steady—his drone rose and fell as each pile was priced. White and red ribbons flew like prizes at the fair. The heavy narcotic scent, so sweet and rich, like incense, and tobacco in shades of gold and amber and mahogany—all precious things, and this was, too. It was marketplace and church rolled together.

"You gettin' back your daddy's allotment?" Mrs. Bellamy gripped him by the elbow and stage-whispered to him.

The two Sidneys were right behind her, the elder fixed on the sale as all the men were, the boy playing a video game. His thumbs jumped, left left right left, and Dave remembered Bert running his thumb down the grip of a new tennis racket as he rolled it in his hand.

"Mrs. Bellamy, I'd like you to meet Tracey Gaines." Tracey smiled and put out her hand, and Mrs. Bellamy took it between both of hers and looked at her deeply. "It's nice to meet you, dear."

"Thank you. I've heard about you from Dave."

"He's like our own. Our own." She let Tracey's hand go with a final pat. They knew who Tracey was and her troubles, of course, more than he had let on, but the Bellamys had the good country manners not to say a word. And of course she was with him. That, too.

"You're looking good," he told Mrs. Bellamy.

"Why, thank you." She pointed at her feet. "It feels so good not to be swole up like I was. I saw Doc Teepen one day and he said, Melva, what have you done to yourself? Next thing I know he's got me prescriptions for water pills and these hose—ain't they pretty?—but they have done wonders."

Dave wondered how long it had been since she'd seen a doctor. His mother had stayed away until she couldn't walk across the room—not that she told him that over the phone. He never knew until he came home from the rehab center how quickly she had failed.

An old black dog with a white chin that had been following the auctioneer came over and flopped with a sigh in front of Tracey. She reached down and patted its head. The dog got back up after a moment as though it had rounds to make, and walked stiff-legged to the next group.

"They let dogs in?" Tracey asked.

"Pretty hard to keep them out," the younger Sidney said, his voice featureless as though it came out of the game that had all his attention.

"Won't it pee on the tobacco?"

"It's a regular, been coming since it was a pup," Dave said, and tried to think how old it was. Fifteen or sixteen, it seemed.

The elder Sidney had gone partway up the rows so he could hear better, and was back now. "Good enough, good enough," he said.

"Last crop?" Dave asked.

"Yep, we're done. Selling off the sticks and wagons—'course we won't get the price we would have five years ago, but there it is. Least ways we won't have to pay to rent those ratty old burlaps anymore."

"David, I wanted to ask your advice on something." Mrs. Bellamy was somber. "He has plans to put in herbs and flowers and all. But

I ponder, why should we rely on selling it down in Raleigh or at the farmers' market? And I can do more than sit in the kitchen and bake biscuits."

"Mommy's got her a plan, too," Sidney said.

"I want him to roll that small barn down by the road, and patch it up nice and fix the door. Then I can make things to sell. Sachets and such."

"She's been reading *Southern Living*," the boy said, like a sleepwalker. She snapped her finger against the back of his head and he half-smiled.

"I think that's a fine idea," Dave told her. He didn't know if it was the medicine or the plans, but she looked ten years younger.

"I have some articles on herb wreaths and herb vinegars," Tracey put in. "I can send them over."

"Bring them over," Mrs. Bellamy said, "when you come visit us with Dave."

Tracey's eyes got wide and moist; she looked about ready to cry. Then he realized that she also had the greenish look of a first-timer around tobacco.

"We will. Soon." He spoke lower to Tracey. "Think we should head out?"

"The smell is strong," she admitted.

"We're going to get some air," he told the Bellamys. "You all take care, now."

"And you take care of that girl of yours," the father said.

They crossed the warehouse, idle leaves that had broken loose skittering across their path. Lester had set up shop on a folding table with a sign taped to the front—LC ENTERPRISES WE BUY LAND! A droopy-looking man and his younger version were just finishing some paperwork. Lester signed with a flourish, then stood to shake their hands and present them each with a business card and a pen.

Dave would have eased by but Lester saw him and came out from behind his table like a bull. He threw his arms out and embraced Dave, and this close the illusion of health faded—he saw the yellow creeping across his eyes, smelled the liquor and foulness on his breath.

"Davy Fordham," he bellowed. "How'd you come by this beauty?"

"This is Lester," he said, extricating himself so he could make introductions. "We were in school together."

Tracey's name didn't come up. He didn't want Lester embarrassing her.

"You have to come down next month for the groundbreaking. Fox Croft. We're gonna have a tent, a pig picking. You come. Even have a band. Biggest one I've done yet—but this," and he waved the newly signed agreement.

Dave didn't ask when. He wanted to get away from Lester, from the future he represented—another farm broken up and the fields planted with cheap white-vinyl houses.

"We have to be going," Tracey said, and he heard in her voice that she knew exactly who this was.

"Sure do. See you."

Lester had been rummaging for an imprinted pen to give them. He held it out, then put it down.

Outside the door, the owner of Leaf Pride II sat on a folding chair, head down and hands hanging between his knees.

"I feel so bad for him," Tracey said.

Dave opened the car door. "Lester?"

"No, him." She looked back at the owner. "If there aren't going to be any more auctions. I guess it's all done."

Now Dave felt the sting in his own eyes, that Tracey could summon care about this stranger and his bankrupt hopes. He sat down and pulled the seat belt across, as though it could hold in both the joy and sadness.

CHAPTER TWENTY

The deputy came out, setting his black hat back firmly on his head. It was the same one from that night, the sergeant who had block-printed her answers as the heater blew stale air around the cruiser. He didn't seem to see her—distracted or maybe not wanting conversation. Or connection.

Tracey watched him head down the hallway to the back stairs and the jail. She knew where the courthouse entrances were, now, a kind of experiential knowledge she'd never expected to gain. She had been there since 8:30, ready to be called before lunch, but some kind of court emergency intervened and things started late. The bench where she waited wasn't built for comfort. She turned, sitting sidesaddle to ease her back, and went back to folding and refolding the handkerchief she'd pulled from the dresser that morning—a fine linen handkerchief, with lace edging, some Southern ladies' once-upon-a-time bought at the antique mall. Tissues would never hold up today.

Prepared as she was, Tracey startled nonetheless when the bailiff poked her head out and stage-whispered, "Miz Gaines!"

She followed her in, aware of the creaking doors behind her, aware of the great space flooded with grainy light from the dome and high windows. The bench was high and dark, the judge perched below a mural of Moses the lawgiver. The bailiff opened the gate to the witness box and Tracey walked up the two steps and turned to face the courtroom.

Ervin Dupree sat alone at a table with a thick book and a thin manila file in front of him. On the other side sat Artis in a blue suit, beside a lawyer who looked like he came from somewhere other than Saul County. Behind them a columned balustrade closed off the place of justice from the audience—rows of wooden seats, dark and glossy as chocolate, curving back and back. Only the first ones were full: Mike Keener, looking almost prosperous, and a couple of reporters with notebooks. No cameras. Then Dave sitting beside Gloria, who'd come in from the country, and Ellen Friedlander—Tracey was surprised to see her, since she had made so little effort to return Ellen's early efforts at friendship. Artis's mother with Jim. Lakesha's family she recognized from the funeral. A few scattered others. Overhead, in a balcony with straight chairs, sat a worn blond woman in a custodian's uniform. Tracey realized she had expected her to be black.

They all seemed like strangers. Even Dave, his kind face creased with concern, was so far away from her place high and apart. A witness. The bailiff held out a black Bible and she rested her hand where a thousand sweaty palms had been. "The truth, the whole truth." The judge rustled on her right. On her left the jury box was empty—the lawyers had agreed to a bench trial, without what Dupree had called "the unknown quantity of the jury." It made it all seem like a show trial, something Soviet, the judge stout and square-headed like Khrushchev.

Dupree walked her through her testimony, following the same laboriously prepared path as the deposition made weeks ago. The facts were familiar. Fact, the school bus stopping. Fact, the dogs running across the field. Fact, Lakesha hopping off the last step and going back to the row of mailboxes.

She saw the dogs break into a run as they crossed the road behind her car. She looked over, expecting to see deer in the plowed field on the other side, but it was empty.

The school bus lurched forward, over the rise. She let off the brake, wanting to be home.

Movement caught her eye again; the dogs were running hard.

Lakesha dawdled up the sand road, swinging her book bag by its strap.

She gained confidence as Dupree continued. He had the

reassuring cadence of a preacher at a Sunday service. There was nothing to fear, just tell the truth. The dogs leaping, Lakesha going down. Tracey's eyes were hot and she swallowed to open a path for the words. She had tried to alert someone or frighten off the pack. Then she went to call for help.

"Thank you, Miz Gaines." He almost bowed.

The defense lawyer rose, bent close to Artis with the air of an old friend. Maybe he was from Charlotte. As he strolled forward Tracey noticed how elegant he was, how closely his suit fit.

"What time was it when the bus stopped at the Downey Trailer Park road?"

"I don't know exactly. After 4. It's the end of the bus route."

"Was it dark?" His tone was gentle, professorial. A seeker of truth.

"It was still light."

"But it was cloudy, wasn't it? Darker than it would have been at that time, had the sky been clear?"

"Yes." He nodded, apparently pleased with her answer.

"When did you first see dogs, Miss Gaines?"

"The bus had stopped to let off children, next to the last stop."

"And what do you recall about them?"

"There were four dogs. Running across the fields. One of them was a big dark dog."

"And when did you see them next?"

"Lakesha was getting the mail."

"So this was later than before. It was even darker then?"

"I guess. I don't know."

"You had your headlights on?"

"Yes."

"And the bus had its stop lights flashing?"

"Yes. No—the bus had started moving. Just the taillights."

"All that light—wasn't it difficult to see out into the darkness?"

"No. It wasn't that dark."

"I see." Tracey wasn't sure if that was supposed to be a joke. She felt the handkerchief as a tight ball in her hand and she opened her fingers, spread it out on her knee.

"So you saw the dogs coming. What was the child doing?"

Lakesha dawdled up the sand road, swinging her book bag by its strap.

She rolled down the window: "Lakesha!"

The girl waved, then opened up a smile and started back toward the highway. Tracey kept an eye on the dogs, worried they would knock her down.

"Hey, dogs!" She yelled, and whistled, but the dogs didn't heed. They angled toward the girl, and now Lakesha saw them.

"She was walking up the road."

"And she threw something at the dogs."

"I called to her and when she saw the dogs running after her, she threw her book bag down."

The lead dog snatched it up, shook it hard one time the way dogs kill groundhogs, one hard snap, then tossed it aside.

The car had drifted almost into the ditch. She turned the wheel and hit the gas, honked the horn, screamed as Lakesha stumbled backward, fell.

"And then she ran."

"She fell down. They attacked her."

"Miss Gaines, one question at a time, please."

"She ran. And she fell down."

The defense attorney was close now, almost leaning into the witness box. His thinning gray hair was combed back from his forehead and the comb had left neat parallel tracks.

"So out there in the dark, beyond your lights, beyond the bus lights, some dogs attacked the girl." His tone shifted, was accusatory, sharp. "How were you able to identify these shadowy dogs?"

"I didn't identify them all," she countered. "Just the ones I knew."

"And you were sure about them."

As she opened the door a dog pushed its lug head into the gap, snapping, growling, blood on its brindled muzzle. She slammed the door hard on its skull twice before it howled and retreated.

A dog clawed the fender and lunged into the open window, teeth bared.

"The dogs that came into the car after me, yes, I'm sure. I saw their faces. Their teeth. I saw their collars."

The attorney nodded. He seemed to be trying to find his next question. It would be over soon and she could go down the stairs and out of the focus of all those eyes in the audience.

"What I don't understand, Miss Gaines…. What I imagine most people cannot understand. Why didn't you help the girl? Why didn't you get out? Why didn't you open the door and pull her into the car?" She could hear Dupree objecting. "You are a teacher, in *loco parentis*, yet you abandoned a child, a student, to her death."

"Enough, Mr. Vanpelt." The judge had a surprisingly high voice, a tenor. "You are badgering this witness, as Mr. Dupree was preparing to say." The prosecutor was on his feet, mouth open, leaning on his hands set flat on each side of the folder.

"Withdrawn. Miss Gaines, why did you leave?"

There is no excuse. She wanted to help—she always, always, *always* wanted to help—but she couldn't see Lakesha and it was all out of her control. Sirens rose and fell, coming for Lakesha, coming for her grandmother. Her grandmother's hand had reached for hers as her body slipped toward the shadow it made on the floor. Even if she could have given her hand, it would have been no use—like giving your hand to a person fallen through ice, so heavy with cold and water that a mere touch would pull you there, too, into the dark. Grandmother Flora went from the community hospital to one in Columbus, and Tracey never made that trip, never seeing her again or the way her skin grew thinner and thinner until it let out her entire life.

What she couldn't help, she had to abandon.

"Miss Gaines?"

The lawyer's face came into focus. Narrow, hard, controlled.

"I was afraid."

"Speak up, please."

"I was afraid." It was nothing but cowardice, in the light of day, the light that poured through the streaked windows and sifted through the filth on the stained-glass dome. She was as soiled as that. Tracey felt tears but didn't raise the handkerchief to wipe them away.

"You were afraid of the dogs. You thought you would be attacked." He commiserated with her weakness.

"The dogs tried to attack me. I didn't think I could do anything." She curled her toes inside her shoes until they cramped, and the pain kept her from sobbing out loud. "I went for help. I did what I could."

"No further questions."

Dupree did not ask for anything more. Tracey felt her body was disconnected from her feet as she walked down the steps, between the lawyer's tables, out through a gate with a spring like the one on her screen door. She let it back gently so it wouldn't slam. She saw Mrs. Pennell, who almost seemed to smile at her. Saw Mike scribbling. Saw Dave. Sat down beside him. Dave put his hand on her knee, and when he lifted it away there was a sudden lightness and rush of cool air that carried a dislocating sense of sexual energy. It was the way his hand had lifted from her breast while still maintaining a sense of connection. Tracey felt that, untethered, she could float across the buzzing courtroom.

Her focus came back as she listened to the medical examiner, a surprisingly young man. He seemed polished and prepared, but vague. The girl's death was caused by dogs. Perhaps several dogs. The bites indicated the large size of the animals and that there was more than one, but the bite marks were not conclusive and by the time the dogs were located, two dogs, there was no blood evidence on them.

"Mr. Pennell's dogs."

"Yes."

"So there is no direct evidence that these dogs were the ones involved at all."

"We cannot rule them out."

"Or rule them in."

"Those two were identified."

"By Miss Gaines."

"Yes."

"But not by science."

Tracey breathed what seemed like the first full breath in hours. Her part was done. She touched Dave's arm and he took her hand.

* * * * *

The defense opened with Orenna Sipe.

Maybe she had wanted to wear black, but someone had talked her out of it. She had on a shiny navy blue suit and a small hat, as though she were going to church. When she took her oath, her voice came low but passionate, an affirmation of faith.

The lawyer was tender with her. They talked about her life, where she was from, her struggle to keep her family together. And that led, inevitably, to Lakesha.

"How did you know Miss Gaines?"

"Teacher at the school."

"And she was a neighbor."

Orenna nodded, and they asked her to say yes, out loud, which she did. She kept her head down, staring into her lap.

"Did she ever do neighborly things, for you or your family?"

"She bought a coat."

"A coat?"

"Must be she thought I couldn't provide for my girl. She got her some coat and give it to her."

"Not to you."

"At school. Like she was charity."

"Did Miss Gaines do anything else?"

"She got my car started once."

"So you knew each other, then? She was a neighbor, acted neighborly?"

"Yes." Grudgingly.

"What do you recall about the night when Lakesha died?"

"I come home from the plant. I doubled—"

"Took another person's shift after your own."

"I worked 16 hours."

"When did you finish?"

"Right close on 3."

"And then you went home?"

"I went to the market. Then I come by my cousin's and got the baby and went home."

"And what were you doing then?"

"I put the baby in her crib and I laid down. I just worked double shift. I was tired."

"You were exhausted. So you went to sleep." The lawyer seemed to ponder that. "What woke you up?"

"I heard a siren. Maybe it was part of my dream, I was laying there and waiting for it to go on by but it didn't. Then I seen lights."

"You never heard a horn?"

"No, sir."

"Did anyone knock on your door?"

"Nobody come. I was asleep right there. I roused up when the siren stayed going and the lights, and I went to look, maybe a wreck on the road. And I seen the police car, and Miz Gaines' car, and I don't see Lakesha."

"But you had a mother's intuition."

"Objection."

"Let me rephrase. You knew something was wrong, and that it might involve your child."

"I come out on the stoop and I look. Where is Lakesha? I knowed my baby was hurt. I run down there and they's bringing her out of the ditch, all bloody. They wouldn't let me get to her." She wiped her hand across her eyes.

"Did you see the dogs?'

"No dogs."

"Did you speak with your daughter?"

"When they let me get in the ambulance she was gone. Already gone."

"Your daughter had passed."

"I never said goodbye to my baby. She didn't give me that." Orenna raised her head and stared straight at Tracey. The same molten stare. Tracey felt her breath held in her throat and she made herself exhale. "I woulda throwd those dogs off her. Any proper woman would, with my bare hands." Orenna lifted her strong hands in testimony, laid them down on the rail of the witness box. "Miz Gaines, she needed you to help her. And then you didn't even come get me, my car in the yard, I was there, you come get me and at least I see my girl before she's gone."

If she had any tears left, she didn't show them now, but with the words out, Orenna seemed to shrink. The anger that had swelled her with menace like a puff adder disappeared and she huddled in her suit.

The defense attorney ran a hand through his hair, paused dramatically, and said there was nothing more.

Dupree had no questions.

Orenna walked out of the courtroom without a glance at anyone.

Tracey felt like she'd been beaten. She hadn't expected to see

Orenna testify. There was no purpose except to make her look bad, and that must have worked. She could feel the eyes on her. Dupree had said she could stay in the courtroom after her testimony, unless there was an objection, but now she wished she had gone home and let this unfold without her.

"The defense recalls Kevin Quarles, the Saul County animal control officer."

He must have appeared before she had. Tracey wondered, as the heavyset man ambled forward, what he had said.

"Mr. Quarles. You testified earlier that the insurance industry has named nine breeds of dogs as high risk—the Staffordshire terrier, boxer, pit bull, chow, Doberman, German shepherd, Great Dane … help me recall."

"And Rottweiler and Siberian husky."

"Isn't it true that most dog bites come not from these breeds, unfairly targeted for their mere names, but from such common pets as the cocker spaniel and Labrador retriever?"

"There's probably more of them around."

"How many dog bites do you think happen each year?"

"I don't know, offhand."

"The Centers for Disease Control and Prevention estimate about 4.5 million dog bite cases each year. But only 12 incidents result in a death. So a dog owner would be highly unlikely to think his dogs, even large dogs, would be dangerous."

"Unless the dog had a history."

"Every dog's allowed one bite, is that the rule?'

"I guess." The man squirmed in his seat.

"Did the dogs Jim Pennell had, the ones he played with, have a history?"

"No, no complaints."

"No biting. No chasing. Nothing."

"That we knew of."

"And the county's regulations, as they existed at the time of the incident, required dogs to be leashed only in towns, incorporated areas."

"Correct."

"Nothing further."

Dupree sighed like a man deeply aggrieved. He walked forward and paused halfway to the witness.

"Mr. VanPelt has been reading up on these sad cases. So have I. According to the Humane Society, the typical biting dog is not some feral creature, half wolf. It's a family pet. Most times a child is bitten. And most attacks occur close to the owner's property. Was that the case here?"

"The houses are on different roads, but the properties adjoin. That's farmland, there's some room out there."

"Yes, yes indeed. Do you like cars, Mr. Quarles?"

The man broke into a smile. "Sure do."

"What's the relative capability of, say, a Volkswagen and a Ferrari? In terms of power, speed."

"Well, that's obvious."

"So you should take more care driving when you have a Ferrari than when you have a little ol' Beetle?"

"Relevance?" The defense attorney was on his feet.

"I have arrived, Your Honor, if you'll permit."

The judge waved him on.

"Mr. VanPelt warns us of the danger of wiener dogs and toy poodles, but surely we recognize the relative danger presented by a large and powerful animal compared with a lapdog. The jaws of a pit bull can exert nearly 1,500 pounds of pressure per square inch. Much like the difference between that VW and that sports car."

"You never can tell about a dog."

"I'd agree with that. Tell me, Mr. Quarles: Saul County regulations state that the animal need not be leashed outside the town limits."

"It does now. They changed that law."

"But at the time of the attack."

"Correct."

"But the law also states that the owner must keep the animal confined to his property or maintain control over it?"

"Yes."

"Did Mr. Pennell have control when these dogs were running wild?"

"Objection."

"So noted."

"Was there any indication that Mr. Pennell had control of his dogs when they were out of his sight?"

"No."

"It is ancient law, common law, that the owner is responsible for damage caused by his hirelings or his creatures. If a cow eats up the corn in your garden or if a dog kills your sheep—the owner is responsible for the damages."

"I'm no lawyer," he protested.

Dupree walked back to his table and brought back the leather-covered book. He appeared triumphant as he asked the man to read the marked section, which he did.

"No further questions."

The courtroom was silent. Tracey remembered how silent it had been that night. The dogs loping across the field, with one big black dog in the lead. They ran like in an old movie, like wolves over the ice in a Russian novel, their bodies rocking forward, heads down.

It was late in the day when Artis was called. The judge hadn't changed his expression through any of it, whether the testimony was routine or emotional, sometimes even seeming to doze. Once she had leaned over to Dave and whispered her suspicions as the judge propped his chin on his hands. Some of the audience had drifted away after hearing the mother.

Artis identified his dogs, in blown-up pictures of them riding in the back of his truck or rolling on the lawn with his son.

"Never had a bit of trouble with them, from pups," he said. "They'd come up missing sometimes, for a day or two, running deer or after a female I guess, but they came home and I never had one complaint about them."

He talked about his divorce, his son, moving back to the farm and buying the puppies to protect his aged mother and his young son.

Tracey heard the sounds of fangs against the car door, wondered if he could imagine his pets that night.

"Has your son adapted well to the rural life?" the defense attorney asked.

"He's had some problems. Sometimes I can't get him to go to school. They put him in the special school and that makes it worse."

"And that's how you came to know Miss Gaines? From the school?"

"Yeah. And you run into folks around Taberville, what there is of it."

"Did she neighbor at your place?"

"We weren't exactly neighbors." He glanced toward her, icy eyes. "And no, she never came by."

"But she knew your dogs."

"Everybody did. They rode around with me all the time."

"Do you think she knows your dogs well enough to identify them?"

Dupree objected, but Tracey wondered how many times you could object and not have the ideas stick.

"Do you know of any reason she would have to make this claim, other than knowing the dogs?"

Tracey felt the focus shift in the room, even the judge seeming to open his weary eyes to consider her. Artis looked down from the witness box and she felt the room begin to swim, her body floating again. *Then Dave will know, everyone will know. There will be nothing left.*

He cleared his throat. The lawyer waited.

"I wouldn't know what goes through a woman's head."

She didn't know whether to bless him for his restraint or hate him for the dismissal in his tone. Maybe it was that Southern thing that kept him from exposing all her failure.

That was the end of it. No more witnesses. She expected the judge would send them home and ponder the evidence, but he spent only a minute or two jotting notes and then asked the defendant to rise.

"On the single count of involuntary manslaughter, the court finds the accused, Artis Pennell, innocent."

He turned to look at his mother and son, seeming to barely restrain a grin.

"The state has failed its essential task of proving that Mr. Pennell's dogs were in fact the culprits, relying on the testimony of a single witness. In addition, county regulations as they then existed did not require these animals be confined, so there is no negligence.

"The court rules that the dogs be returned to the Pennell family."

Tracey drew in a breath. "However, given the uncertainty as to whether they may have been involved in this fatal attack, and in light of new county regulations, they are to be leashed or penned at all times."

The gavel came down.

Tracey let Dave steer her out of the courtroom. He gripped her forearm and leaned close, so that she had to match her steps to his, but she would have moved no faster in any case. "It's over," he whispered. "It's over."

Keener was waiting just outside the double doors.

"Do you have anything to say about the verdict?" His eyes were bright, eager, and Tracey just stared at him. He wore a better suit now but he was the same man, the reporter insinuating himself with a source. Just because he was an outsider like her did not make him an ally.

She shook her head. His professional demeanor never wavered as he moved past her to the Pennell family, coming out with big smiles.

"I'd watch outside," he offered. "The TV people are waiting."

"Wouldn't want them to get what he didn't," Dave observed. "Let's take the back stairs."

At the landing, they came upon Orenna Sipe and another woman. They appeared to be praying, right there in the courthouse. They looked up at the clanging on the metal staircase.

Tracey stopped, then started down. She wanted to tell Orenna that she understood, now.

Orenna watched her approach. Her eyes were no longer crackling with anger, or molten with hurt.

"Mrs. Sipe …"

She raised her hand, warning or benediction, and turned away without a word.

No easy forgiveness to be had. Maybe tolerance. As she stood alone with her need, Tracey felt Dave's hand on her shoulder, and looked back to see Gloria was behind him, and Ellen. She didn't really hear what they had to say. It was enough to be surrounded by their voices.

CHAPTER TWENTY-ONE

Dave raised the shades on the windows so that the class would be greeted by a bright morning when they arrived, instead of stewing in the dull yellow light. The room faced west, and afternoon sun poured through as each shade rattled up, spearing across the floor and highlighting the dust set awhirl by his movement. He dropped the class roster into his bag and clicked the latches, pushed his chair in to the desk. He had dinner duty tonight, a couple of rib-eyes to grill and a salad. Tracey had gone to the store for a bottle of wine. There wasn't much to celebrate, but at least there was an end.

Someone pounded toward his door, followed immediately by another runner, and then the unmistakable sound of a body being slammed into the metal lockers across the hall.

"Motherfucker!"

"Yeah? Yeah?" Another bang as he reached the door.

Jim had another boy up against the wall, holding him by the shoulders and slamming his head against the locker. He couldn't think of his name, something, a holiday. Christmas. No, Easter. A new kid, big, shaved bald. Trouble.

"Stop that!" he said, and Jim turned just enough to loosen his grip. The other kid yanked loose and dived under Jim's arms, came up with a hard punch that sent Jim staggering back into Dave.

He pushed away and windmilled toward his opponent, but the

other boy just seemed to shrug off the blows and then sent a powerful punch into Jim's stomach.

That took some of the fight out of him. Dave used the opening to pull him away. "Jim, come on."

But Jim wasn't hearing anything. He stiffened under Dave's touch.

"Nigger," he said, not even in anger, just as a statement. "Dirt-dumb country nigger."

Easter began to flail as wildly as Jim had. Dave heard the crunch of cartilage as a fist caught Jim's ear, tried to push his arm between them and then another fist came across and met his jaw.

"Damn it!" Pain shot across his split mouth. The boys stopped then, frozen by the sight of a teacher bleeding.

"Ford—ham—hey." Tick Newhouse caught his breath between each syllable. "You—o—kay?"

"Yeah. Hold on there a minute." He grabbed Jim, who had started to slide away, and Newhouse grabbed Easter.

"I called—the SRO," Newhouse said. Dave wondered how long he'd been chasing them, though it wouldn't take much effort to get the pudgy biology teacher in this state.

"Let me talk to this one." Dave jerked his head toward his classroom and Jim, his face blotchy with rage, went sullenly inside and slammed himself down at a desk. He took his time closing the door, lining out what he might say.

"This ended ugly, but I don't imagine it started with much. What got you two going?" He greatly wanted to sit down behind his desk to cover the shaking in his knees, but that would put too much wood and distance between them. Instead, he stood and rested his hands on the chair back.

Jim hung his head and let his hair fall to cover his face. His ear was red, heading toward purple, but not bleeding.

"Easter is new," Dave observed. He tried to pull out the side drawer and it stuck, as usual, until he pulled it free with a squeal. He took out a tissue and dabbed at his mouth. It hurt. *Why on earth he'd gotten between those two young fools.* "Maybe he said something, trying to establish himself? His propers, as you say?"

Jim turned in the chair, as far as it would let him, and stared at the back wall.

He was ready to let the whole mess go, let the SRO handle it. The hope he'd had for Jim was all gone, erased by his actions over the past few months. The boy who had curled a tentative arm around his paper had burned away to become this lean, simmering youth, and just for a minute he felt a jolt of familiar fear. But he heard an old teacher in Durham, rubbed smooth by his battles but also polished by them: "If you succeed with one student, then you can count yourself a success as a teacher."

"I was surprised to hear the N-word coming from you," he tried again. Jim put his hand over his bruised ear. "That's not the Jim Pennell I knew last fall. Not the one I thought would be out of here come this fall."

"I woulda been, if you'da given me a C."

He let it pass. Jim knew better than to try that subject. The English D only reinforced the rest of his grades.

Dave came around and sat on the corner of the desk. Make contact. Cross the gulf.

"Whatever he said, or you said, it's not worth the consequences."

"How would you know?" Jim raised his head and glared. "If you don't fight back, they'll run over you. You have to stand up for yourself."

He surely couldn't imagine how deep that cut.

"Sometimes you do," he said, trying to thread the path between the boy's hurt and his own, and something that went deeper. "Think about someone you know who's had to stand up and be strong. Who had to do what was right when everyone seemed to be against her."

Jim scowled at the last word.

"When you ran four-wheelers around her house and tore up her lawn and frightened her. When you let the air out of her tires downtown. When you keyed her car."

Jim's arms were rigid, his hands clenched around the sides of the desk.

"Screw her."

"She stood up for herself."

"She's a troublemaker." Dave heard the father behind every word. "We didn't have enough trouble anyway."

Jim shoved out of the desk, sending it skidding across the floor.

"This shithole place! I hate it. I hate being here. Here in the sticks. Why couldn't we stay in Charlotte? I had friends there, not these dirtballs. Rejects." He paced as he talked, toward the windows, then back toward the door. "I'll never fit in here. You understand? Never. I don't want to."

Dave stood away from the desk. He should be afraid of Jim, his newly gained size and his reach, his anger focused on everyone and no one, but instead he found himself getting calm and centered.

"You." Jim came up close. He had shaved fast and poorly. His jaw line was scraped and streaks of uneven stubble showed. Dave smelled cinnamon gum. "You're just the zookeeper. All of you. That's what you think. We're the animals. Freaks." And he made a gargoyle face.

"None of us fit in, Jim. No one does. We're all out of place, until we decide that this is our place." He began to see where he was going, gained surety as he did. "I know how the kids laugh at me, Gimpy, because I walk with a limp. You ever wonder why?"

Jim didn't move or nod, but his glance shifted to Dave's feet, then back.

"You asked, how would I know, about fighting back, or not. OK, this is what I know about fighting."

He sat on the corner of the desk and pulled up his pant leg. The exposed brace was as shocking as an entirely artificial limb, a construction of leather and beige plastic and metal, a carapace that shielded the soft tissue inside.

"I wasn't born like this. I was like you. I worked tobacco, ran, played ball." Jim sniffed. "I grew up here and went to school here, and I was on the tennis team and good enough to win trophies if you ever look in the case at the school board office."

"So you got hurt. Big deal."

"I didn't *get hurt*. Didn't wreck a car or anything like that." Dave almost stopped. What he told Jim would be fodder for the kids, for all of them to repeat. The taunts would be worse. He started again. "I was teaching at an inner-city school in Baltimore. Walking home, getting dark. Winter time. I ran into a group of gang members, who apparently didn't want to be seen right then."

"And they jumped you."

"They beat me."

"Wrong place, wrong time." Jim threw that out with the same attitude.

"They punched me until they got me down, and then they kicked me. I was down in the gutter, in the snow. Then one of them picked up an iron pipe. And he hit my leg, and hit my leg, and hit my leg, and hit my leg."

"God," Jim breathed.

"I didn't want to fight back, because they were kids. And then I couldn't fight back. But the worst damage they did wasn't to my insides or head or leg. That was bad enough. What they did was make me scared."

Now it was Dave's turn to pace, because he couldn't tell this and look at Jim, face the mingled awe and disgust he saw in his eyes.

"By the time I got out of the hospital, I was afraid to stay in the city. I was afraid of young black men, and that made me ashamed of myself, because I knew better. Was raised better. Because it was a black man who was brave enough to pick me up out of the gutter and get help. So I came home, Jim."

"At least you have a home."

"It wasn't home any more. I lived in the same house with my mother, went to the same places. Didn't matter—the place was the same, but I was changed. It's hard to come to someplace new and not fit in, I know that, but it maybe is worse to come back to where you're from and not fit in there anymore."

Jim was staring at him, his lips moving a little as though he wanted to say something. His shoulders had gone slack.

"Well, that's about it." Dave grabbed his satchel and was surprised that his hand was steady. "You ready?"

Jim's mouth began to shudder and his eyes were wide. And then he was crying, tears brimming over and rolling down his cheeks; he stood motionless until Dave dropped his bag and went to put an arm around his shoulders.

Jim threw his arms around Dave and held on like a man in a storm holding onto a far too slender tree.

"I did it," he whispered.

"It doesn't matter." Whatever it was, whatever petty meanness to Tracey, didn't matter.

"It *does*. I was rotten. If I'da been better, she wouldn't have gone and left Dad. It was my fault."

Dave felt the world shift a little. "You don't have to take that on yourself. Whatever happened was about her and your dad, not you. It's that way. It's about the husband and wife, not the kids."

Dave felt a shudder run through Jim. "I miss her," he said. "I do. I miss Mom even if Dad hates her."

A knock on the door scared them both. Jim pulled back, rubbed his face on his sleeve. "Mr. Fordham." It was the school officer. "Mr. Fordham?" The door started to open.

"Just a minute."

Jim wiped his face again and sucked in a big breath.

"You OK?" Dave asked, and Jim nodded.

"I'm coming in." The door rattled again and Dave stepped over and opened it, nearly pulling Buckner into the room.

Easter was sitting on the floor against the lockers. Tick stood to one side, as though he were guarding.

"He tells me things got a bit sideways here." Buckner stared at Dave's face.

"Yeah, a brush-up." He'd almost forgotten the split lip.

"Someone hit you?"

"It was an accident. I got in the way."

"I see blood, I figure it's more than an accident. We gotta get them down and do the report."

Jim hung his head. Dave wanted to say something more, but he couldn't undo what the two had started. Easter scrambled to his feet and they headed downstairs, the SRO at the back like he was herding them along.

"There'll be automatic suspension. I'll need you to make a statement, so they can decide the rest."

"I know. In a minute."

Dave went down to the bathroom and checked out the damage. The blood had dried in a black line and his lip was puffy, but it wasn't too bad. He splashed cold water against his face until it stopped stinging, and dried off with the stiff brown paper towels from the dispenser.

He looked again, and the face that looked back—despite the

fading hair, the tired eyes—wasn't so much different from the one that used to face him in a high school bathroom just like this. The flickering fluorescent bulb, the glossy brown paint on the stall doors covering years of graffiti, the cracked tiles. Landscape with Davy Fordham, then and now.

He went back to his room and gathered up his things. The worn leather bag didn't look much like the stiff new satchel his mother gave him to start at Carolina. He liked it better this way, scuffed and abraded. Wearing the impress of years.

Buckner's door was closed when he went by, though he could hear them talking inside. Morning was soon enough for statements.

As he started down the steps, something made him turn back. The light was rich and golden on the legend above the door: Truth is strong and will prevail.

Maybe not in court. He went down the formal staircase, step and drag, step and drag. But some ways, sometimes, it does.

CHAPTER TWENTY-TWO

The hinge of the year—can't you hear them, sweetie? A squeaky old hinge."

Tracey watched the grackles wheel towards the woods to roost, their grating voices blended into a rusty chorus. Her grandmother had looked up and said that each year, watching them flock, as she had her sayings for the killdeer arriving in spring and the whippoorwills calling on summer nights.

Dave stopped beating the other end of the Persian carpet and followed her attention.

"Grackles," he said.

"Um-hmm. Grandma Flora called them the hinge of the year. Fall."

"I guess." He whacked the rug and dust came away, to be swept up in the breeze. "For me, it's always the geese, the Canadas. Not the local flocks but the ones from up north, flying high at night and honking. That's fall."

She hit the carpet again with the two-by-four—not much of an implement, but available—and wondered if they'd ever get the dust and dirt out. Some of it probably went back decades; though she'd thought her vacuuming had done the job, Dave warned that only hauling them outside and beating them in the traditional manner would free up what clung inside the weft.

The grackles funneled into the woods like a tornado touching down. Everything whirled, the dust, leaves fallen from the persimmon and pecan and willow oaks. Everything seemed to recall something else. It was the nostalgia that came with the year shutting down, she supposed. She thought of Thanksgiving, the cold floor, lying on her stomach watching *The Wizard of Oz* when the scenes were still fresh enough to make her hang onto her pillow. The tornado didn't scare her—she'd watched the real thing often enough, distant funnels twisting across the horizon—but the haunted forest, the flying monkeys, the lit broom as it touched the Scarecrow's straw. When the story came back to Kansas she always felt a great relief to be home again, in a tall house like her grandmother's, set out in the cropland.

"Think that's enough?" Dave stepped back, balanced himself, and wiped his sleeve across his brow.

"What do you think?'

"I think."

They hauled the rug off the clothesline and lugged it up the porch and into the parlor. The maroons and greens looked cleaner, the cream parts definitely. She guessed he was right. And it smelled cool like the outside. The claw feet of the settee went back onto the edge of the rug and they lifted the tables back into place and set the lamps on them and lighted them. The sky was still bright through the half-bare trees but the shadows were long across the lawn.

"I forgot to tell you." Dave was headed back for the small rug and she followed. "I ran into Trey down in Raleigh. He's enrolled in a GED class through the community college."

"That's good. I hope he sticks."

"Me, too."

She wondered at the strong affirmation in his voice. Trey had only impressed her as a thug in training. Dave seemed to put so much more stock in these kids than she did.

Garland was sitting in his usual spot on the porch railing. Tracey sat down near him and stroked his rough back. He didn't lift himself against her hand, or purr, just opened and closed his eyes. Dave pulled the small fringed rug from the line and carried it back over one arm, using the two-by-four as a walking stick as he crossed the lawn. Garland opened his eyes at the approaching steps. Dave rested his palm on the cat's broad head, for reassurance, and scratched behind his ears. The cat bent his head one way and then the other, then moved back to resettle in his own space.

He had a real sense of himself—the first time she'd seen him, Garland had taken no more note of her than a fox on its rounds. She had found the teaching job and was chasing around with a real estate broker during Easter holiday break. This place was well down the list. Too big, too isolated, dirty from the last tenants. She was standing in the kitchen, looking out the window left open to clear the musty smell, sure she couldn't face the cracked bathroom or ripped-out mantel in the parlor. Such a big, echoing place to fill. A black-and-white cat came from behind one of the sheds and trotted into the open. Tracey made the mouse-squeak that cats always noticed, but this one just kept moving, neither faster nor slower.

"There's some feral cats around," the agent said apologetically.

"I see." But she was encouraged at the cat's assured presence. He lived here, or she, whatever. There was a spirit, some life. She took the house, moved down at the end of the school term and threw herself into cleaning and fixing. Silly, perhaps, to care about some wild cats, but at the time she thought she could bring them back into the civilized world. Only Garland was willing. The others remained wild, more aloof than barn cats that at least knew how the milk got into the pans and acknowledged their connection. These cats came like raccoons, eating and then gone. Gradually they had drifted away. Celia had a brood of kittens and disappeared. Enoch had a torn ear that made him drop his head and shake it—then he was gone.

"Honey?"

Dave was waiting on her.

He waited as she put down the waffle mat that held the rug to the pine boards. As she adjusted the lay of the rug, he brought the plant stand back to its place. They moved around each other—already a shared life.

How unexpected. She'd thought she was happy in her busyness before, the hard work of cleaning and repairing, the nights grading papers while the rain drove on the tin roof. Her occasional restlessness was no more than the biological drive for sex, no more than that—after Carl, she'd sworn off the idea of another relationship.

She watched Dave shift a small picture from one table to another, turning it to face the room. Some of his things were among hers now, his books, some antiques that came each with its own history. He moved around his limp with a certain grace—that would never change, it was as much a part of him as the way fine hair curled at the base of his spine. As much as the memories that defined both of them.

"How's that?" He swept his arm to indicate the room. Tracey saw him as a stranger, barely known—was she settling too fast, giving in too easily to future heartache?—then he gave that wide-open smile.

"I like it."

"Good, because I think I'm done for tonight. What's for dinner?"

"Stir-fry or frozen pizza."

"OK. You want me to start the rice?"

It was stir-fry, then. With Carl, it would have been a push and pull, what do you want, no, what do you want? There was a sureness between them, a quiet that went beyond intellectual meshing. Affinity. His protective aloofness, her tight control that kept her moving after her grandmother, after Carl, after Lakesha—when her whole spirit wanted to just lie down and give up. Each winter, up north, drivers would go off the road or hunters take the wrong trail in the national forest, struggle, get drowsy and warm, and lie down and die. You had to keep moving. It was easy to freeze to death. That wasn't something people understood here.

She followed him into the kitchen and starting rattling through the usual pans to reach the wok. Dave stood at the sink.

"Someone's coming."

"Huh?"

He pointed up the road and now she heard it, too, an engine gunning up the lane, the thump and rattle as the tires hit hard on the ruts.

They went out onto the porch. A truck showed through the trees—red.

"Damn it," she said.

"Artis."

"What's this about?"

Dave moved forward, closer to the steps, as the truck wheeled off the track and onto the yard.

Artis turned off the engine and got out, leaving the door open and the warning bell chiming. He went back and dropped the gate, reached in and dragged something toward the back. It was heavy and caught as he pulled, until he yanked and the body of the big brindled dog slid from the bed. He took the collar and pulled the limp body onto the lawn.

"Here," he said, breathing hard. "My son's dog."

He glared up at them. Sweat marked his gray T-shirt.

"I shot it. I shot the damned thing because I couldn't stand its howling any more. Tied up, digging a circle in the dirt, howling all night because you don't tie a living creature up by the neck."

"Artis," Dave cautioned.

"His name was Boomer. Jim named him. Boomer." His voice shook. "He won't have his dog when he comes home from his damn mother's."

"Better he didn't see this," Dave said.

"Yeah. Better. Whatever that means." Artis looked past Dave to Tracey. His face went white. "Better he doesn't have a mother. Better he rots out here. Better he dead-ends in a tobacco field. Better he sees his father arrested and hauled into court. For nothing, for your finger-pointing to cover your own sorry ass."

Dave was saying something, his voice measured and meant to pacify. Tracey felt as though her brain had numbed, the words making no impact or sense.

She watched Garland come from under the bushes and circle the dog's body. The lug head was streaked with blood and that blood smell drew him.

"You've made our lives hell."

"I'm not responsible," she said, not particularly to him, and Dave turned and looked at her.

"You oughta talk about responsible. All fucking ready to run the show, all of you, rule the world, until something happens or something goes wrong, and then you run off and play girl, let it all go to hell while you hide."

"I'm not running." Her voice seemed to come from quite a distance away. Closer, like a whisper in her ear, were the words she didn't say: *I don't need your permission to live here. Not yours, not anyone's.*

"Maybe you ought to." Artis walked back to the truck, leaned across the seat. The truck chimed its flat repetitive chime. The light from the dome gleamed on his hair, his arm, the flat black side of a pistol.

"Get back!" Dave shoved her toward the door and she caught herself on the frame. Artis drew the gun down and shot at the dog, she thought, until she saw Garland's body leap into the air, twist and fall.

Tracey ran, hearing voices behind her. She banged into a table, a chair, slid into the far wall of the parlor and pulled the shotgun from its hooks. She was almost onto the porch when Dave met her.

"I'm not going to let him …"

"Let me," he said, his face altered in a way she didn't recognize. He took the gun.

"You got any more strays?" Artis fired again, toward the shadow of the barn, toward nothing. "How about him?" He waved the pistol at Dave.

Tracey saw Dave raise the shotgun. It sat easily against his shoulder, as it never had on hers. The shape of it was strange as the clear empty sky, the silence, the way the whole evening had seemed to halt right before the shadows took the world.

Artis brought the pistol up and laid it against his chest.

The shotgun was empty. Surely Dave remembered that. She wondered if Artis had more bullets in that pistol, flat as a rattlesnake's head, or if it was empty. She was terrified that he would shoot and also that the two of them would throw aside the weapons and go at each other with fist and foot and tooth. In that moment they were alike, both of them wild, the skin pulled tight on their bones—outside her control or her understanding.

No accounting for them, she heard again, Artis or Dave or the old soldiers under their forgotten stones, all pulled together by being men or being men raised up here on this dirt. It was harder to enter that alien territory than any other.

Dave waited. *How still his face is.* She wanted to move in front of him and protect him from the shot that would inevitably come, but the set of his mouth wouldn't allow her. She couldn't lose him, but she couldn't save him, either.

The dusk-to-dawn light hummed. Artis flinched. The light flickered for a long time, it seemed, strobing him as though in frozen motion, until it steadied and the lawn was a small room in its greenish glow with the night pulled down all around.

Artis let the gun slide a bit, then all the way down his body until it hung in his fingers.

He tossed it beside the dog.

"I'm done," he said, and she believed it, the slope of his shoulders that couldn't hold up any hope. "Done. I'll take Jim somewheres he doesn't have to deal with any of this. And you can perch here, Tracey, forever, until you die, but you won't ever, ever be part of this place."

"That's not true, Artis. She has roots with me. The two of us." Dave tilted his head her way, then back.

The animals lay peacefully together, the dog with its mouth closed, the black-and-white cat draped across its outstretched legs. Blood couldn't be distinguished under the harsh light. The whole scene might have been posed.

Dave went down the steps, his bad foot hitting hard on each one, limped over and picked up the pistol. Artis just stared at the dead things, rage collapsed into grief.

She didn't hear what Dave said to him, but Artis nodded, and Dave set the weapons aside and helped him pick up the dog. They carried it back to the truck by its legs and swung it back and then up onto the tailgate, pushed it out of sight. They stood together at the back of the truck. In a moment they would separate, Dave would come back.

Garland remained. The wildness that had kept him safe, would never have let him come within range, had been given up for a bowl of food and a sunny spot on the porch railing.

Tracey wondered which he would have chosen, had he the choosing.

ACKNOWLEDGMENTS

I am grateful to my classmates and professors in the MFA program at Queens University of Charlotte, who read this book as it grew, chapter by chapter. I appreciate the kind guidance offered by John Banks and the wise counsel of Press 53 publisher Kevin Morgan Watson. And many thanks to the North Carolina Arts Council and the partnering arts councils of the Central Piedmont Regional Artists Hub Program, whose support was instrumental in its completion.

Valerie Nieman
February 2011

VALERIE NIEMAN worked for three decades as a journalist while honing her skills as a poet and fiction writer. She is the author of a collection of short stories, *Fidelities*, from West Virginia University Press, and a poetry collection, *Wake Wake Wake*. She has received an NEA creative writing fellowship, two Elizabeth Simpson Smith prizes in fiction, and the Greg Grummer Prize in poetry. A native of Western New York State, she graduated from West Virginia University and the M.F.A. program at Queens University of Charlotte. She teaches writing at N.C. A&T State University and is the poetry editor for *Prime Number Magazine*.

Photographer **DOROTHY O'CONNOR** graduated from Georgia State University with degrees in Literature and Studio Arts. She continued her education at The Creative Circus, a commercial art school in Atlanta. Her fine art photographs feature thoughtfully composed scenes, combining elements of still-life, portraiture and landscape to produce unique and evocative works of art.

Please visit www.dorothyoconnor.com to view and learn more about her work.

CPSIA information can be obtained at www.ICGtesting.com
Printed in the USA
BVOW02s2325240216

437977BV00002B/31/P